SPORTS SHORTS

Ghost in the Bleachers

AND OTHER BASEBALL STORIES

By David E. Griffith

LOWELL HOUSE JUVENILE

LOS ANGELES

CONTEMPORARY BOOKS

CHICAGO

For my parents, James and Mary Griffith.
Every child should be so fortunate.

"The Trade" was written by Geof Smith

Library of Congress Catalog Card Number: 97-4982
ISBN: 1-56565-620-2

Publisher: Jack Artenstein
Editor in Chief, Roxbury Park: Michael Artenstein
Director of Publishing Services: Rena Copperman
Managing Editor: Lindsey Hay
Art Director: Lisa-Theresa Lenthall
Cover illustration: Mia Tavonatti

Roxbury Park is an imprint of Lowell House,
A Division of the RGA Publishing Group, Inc.

Lowell House books can be purchased
at special discounts when ordered in bulk
for premiums and special sales.
Contact Department TC at the following address:

Lowell House Juvenile
2020 Avenue of the Stars, Suite 300
Los Angeles, CA 90067

Manufactured in the United States of America

10 9 8 7 6 5 4 3 2 1

Contents

Ghost in the Bleachers

Baltimore, Maryland, 1906

"Bang! You're dead."

"No, I'm not! You missed."

The old man watched from the edge of the woods as two boys came running toward him across the clearing. He knew they had come from the old brick school down the street. They were dressed in rough wool pants and dirty white shirts made of raw cotton. Their faces were smeared with dust and sweat.

The larger of the two boys was holding a battered old baseball bat. He was stout, but he was too muscular to be called fat. The old man watched him cradle the beat-up old bat in both hands, raise it to his face, and aim it like a rifle. He was pointing it at the smaller boy, who was holding a bent and gnarled hickory branch. The smaller boy darted to the left into a patch of waist-high grass and weeds, turned around, dropped to one knee, and held his hickory branch in one hand like a bow. He mimed taking an arrow out of an imaginary quiver, fitting it on a nonexistent bow-string, drawing the string, and firing.

They started yelling at each other. "I got you."

5

"No, you didn't. I got you first."

The two boys walked toward each other to continue their argument. "You're a lyin' red Indian, Billy Reily," the larger boy said.

"And you're a lyin' fat bluecoat, Georgie."

Georgie laughed. Any other kid who called him a liar was asking for trouble. He'd fought nearly every boy in school till they cried "Uncle," but never Billy. Despite his tiny frame, Billy wasn't afraid of anybody, and Georgie respected that. Besides, Billy was the only true friend Georgie had, so he decided to let Billy win this time.

"OK, Billy, you got me," Georgie declared, seeing the old man for the first time. He was standing about 20 feet from the boys, watching them curiously.

"Ain't that right, mister," Georgie said, addressing the old man.

"I'm sorry, son. What was the question?"

"He shot me, didn't he?" Georgie asked, winking behind Billy's back and urging the old man to say yes.

"You don't look hit to me," the old man said, shifting his weight on his dark wooden cane.

Georgie laughed.

"Aw, mister, we're only pretendin'," Billy said.

"Oh, I see," the old man said. "Tell me, how do you ever know who won?"

"It doesn't really matter thet much, mister. We're just practicin'."

"It never matters thet much," the old man said under his breath. He looked down at the boys with a grandfatherly smile. "Practicin'. What on earth for, son?"

"Army practicin'," Billy said.

"Well, son, I ain't one to tell a man what to do with his time, but thet seems like a silly thing for two boys to do on such a fine Indian summer day." He stared off into the distance. "Believe me, the Army will come for you soon enough."

"Nah, it won't. We gonna go to *it*," Billy said. "We hear the Army is a grand life for a boy. Our teacher says we'll do nothin' but ride horses, shoot guns, and scrap with Injuns. Stuff like thet." Billy looked excitedly at the old man. "We can't wait, so we're gonna run away and join up. Georgie's gonna be a sergeant and I'm gonna be his, uh—what's thet thing I'm gonna be again, Georgie?"

"Corporal," Georgie replied.

"That's right. I'm gonna be a corporal. We're gonna fight and camp and ride. The Army's gonna be fun, and our teacher says they'll even pay us to do it. Ain't thet great?"

Stroking his white mustache, the old man looked off toward the school, thinking about his response.

"You OK, mister?" Georgie asked.

The old man frowned as he gazed into Georgie's eyes, then shook his head, as if he knew something the boys didn't know. He cleared his throat. "Yeah, I was just thinkin', is all. Look, um…boys, the Army ain't like thet at all."

Georgie looked at the old man and sneered. The old man didn't look like the kind of man who got into many scraps. He was all dandied up in a light gray suit. His mustache was snowy white and neatly trimmed, and his cane was a dark smooth wood with a brass head.

"How you know, you ever been in the Army?" Georgie asked, expecting the answer to be no.

"Yeah, I was in the Army, son. A long time ago."

The old man started to say more, but Billy interrupte

him. "Did you shoot any Injuns, mister?" Billy often looked at the covers of dime novels about Western heroes and cavalry battles against warring Indians at the drugstore down the road from his home. He couldn't read, so his imagination fed off the covers, which often depicted bloody battle scenes.

"Injuns?" The old man almost laughed. "Not that I know of, Corporal. There weren't that many around these parts by then."

"When was that?"

The old man looked tired. Dark circles had formed under his eyes. "I tell you what, boys. I'll tell you all about my Army days on one condition."

"What's thet?" Billy asked.

"Let's go over in the shade. An old soldier like me needs to stay out of the hot sun."

They walked across the clearing toward the woods. The old man needed his cane to walk, and the boys slowed down to stay with him. *Pretty country*, the old man thought, knowing it wouldn't stay that way for long. The city was growing toward these meadows and woods, and soon there would be nothing but brick buildings on the horizon, and all these trees with their red and gold palette of fall colors would be chopped down.

They walked deep into the woods to the point where they could see the little church on the other side. The church was made of old mud brick, faded and yellowed with time. Beside it was a gated cemetery with row upon row of old, weathered stones.

"Let's not go any farther, mister," Billy said.

"Why? What's wrong, son?"

"Billy don't like to go near boneyards," Georgie said. "They scare him."

Billy glared at Georgie and pulled a clump of grass out of the ground in front of him.

The old man put a hand on Billy's shoulder. "Ain't nothin' in a cemetery to be afraid of, son. Just folks who've passed on is all."

"Mama says there's devils in the boneyard," Billy said, hoping the old man would refute this claim.

The old man sighed. "OK. We can sit here." Using his cane for support, he eased his weight onto an old fallen tree at the fringe of the woods, wincing from the pain in his knees and back. "Tell me something, boys. You got thet bat there, how come you ain't playin' ball?"

"We ain't got no ball, mister," Georgie said.

"Thet right? Well, you know, a lot of boys have played ball near these woods. They may've lost one in here. Keep your eyes open and you might just find one." Trying to sound enthusiastic, he slapped an open hand on his thigh and gave a wide smile.

"Now, sit down, boys, and I'll tell you 'bout my Army days. First of all, what are your names?"

"This is Georgie, and I'm Billy Reily, but you can call me Corporal. I like that."

"Glad to meet you, Corporal. I'm Captain Josiah Martin," the old man said heartily, reaching out his open hand.

"A captain! Wow! Who'd you fight?" Georgie asked.

The old man took a small enamel pin off the lapel of his light gray suit and dropped it into Georgie's hand.

Georgie and Billy studied the pin. It was blue enamel with red letters reading GAR.

"GAR? What's that, mister?" Billy asked.

"Grand Army of the Republic," Captain Martin said. "It means I fought for the gov'ment in the War of the Rebellion. What some folks call the Civil War."

Georgie looked down at the pin with new respect. He rubbed its enamel face against his palm and handed it back to the old captain. The captain pinned it back on his lapel. "Well, lessee. I guess I should start at the beginnin'. Back in 1860 I was nineteen, going to that school right down the street here. My folks thought I was there studyin' to be a doctor, but all I really was doin' was playin' ball. Me and Jim Chandler, we were the best players on the team."

The boys started to fidget, anxious to hear about the Army.

Captain Martin continued. "Jim could hum that ball right past anybody, no matter how hard they swung at it. I was the best hitter on the team, but even I couldn't touch Jim's fastball. We played other teams at other schools. It wasn't very organized or nothin', but it was fun, and nobody ever got hurt—at least not bad. And no matter what happened, I could count on Jim. We was thick, me and him."

"C'mon, mister, get to the good stuff," Georgie said, pulling his feet closer to his body.

"Son, this is my story," the captain said angrily. "I'll decide how to tell it. All right?"

The boys glanced at each other, then looked down at the ground.

"Anyway," the captain continued, "me and Jim, we was the best of friends. But then we changed. The whole world changed. It changed when Mr. Lincoln became president." The old man stroked his mustache and looked thoughtfully at the boys. "Now, I loved Mr. Lincoln. I cried when he was killed. But them folks down South hated him so much, they decided to form their own country. That was a bad time, boys. It was a bad time for Maryland. See, many of the folks round these parts were for the South, and the rest of us were for the North. People fought in the streets; people beat each other up. It was a bad time."

Georgie picked up the bat and laid it across his lap, twisting it around unconsciously. "It was a bad time for me and Jim, too," the old man said. "I always knew thet Jim's folks was from Virginnie, but I never thought nothin' about it. Thet spring of 1861 I *had* to think about it. Jim went and volunteered to fight for them damned Rebels, and I did the same for the gov'ment. I didn't see him again for over two years. It wasn't till after Gettysburg. . . ."

The boys got excited. They weren't good students—never paid attention in school—but they knew about Gettysburg. "Gettysburg? You was at Gettysburg, mister?" Georgie asked. "That was a big scrap." He looked up at the captain with renewed respect.

"Ain't no big thing, boys. More'n a hundred fifty thousand men was at Gettysburg, and thet don't even include the people who lived in thet poor little town. But, yes, I was there, and so was Jim. He was in one of those Virginnie units that got cut to pieces on the third day. Somehow he managed to survive, and he and the rest of the Reb army retreated back into the South. We didn't chase them, we just licked our wounds and gave them time to get strong again. We shoulda gone after 'em, but we didn't."

"Was it scary bein' in a scrap like thet?" Georgie asked.

12

"It was scarier than anything you can imagine. And it was tirin'. We fought all day till dark for three days. And the whole time it was so hot, I could barely breathe."

Georgie and Billy hung on every word. The old man rubbed his eyes. "Gettysburg was, like you said, a big scrap. And not much happened thet fall. The fight had been knocked out of both armies, blue and gray, and we just camped and marched and marched and camped. The one thing they never tell boys like you about war is how borin' it is. Being in a war is terrible borin'. We was in combat ten days in 1863. Ten terrible, bloody days, but just ten days all the same. Thet's ten out of three hundred sixty–five. The rest of the year was spent campin' and marchin' when we weren't sick, and we was sick all the time. Army food is terrible, boys."

"Couldn't be worse than the slop they serve us here at school," Billy said.

"You'd be surprised," the old man said. "Anyway, thet fall of 1863, we was in camp near the Reb lines on some ugly river in northern Virginia. Nothin' had happened for weeks. And the weather was really pretty. Much like today, come to think of it. It was Indian summer and warm and clear with just a hint of winter comin'. Private Wilkens come up to me and said our camp guards—we called 'em pickets—had been talkin' to the Reb camp guards, and they wanted a truce, so they could go swimmin' without getting shot. I didn't see no harm in it, so I agreed."

A bee buzzed past Billy's ear. He got up and started swatting at it. Captain Martin stopped talking, and Georgie chuckled. "You think it's so funny, why don't I swat it over to you, and you can let it sting your butt," Billy said to Georgie.

"Sit down and leave it alone, or it's gonna sting you," the old man said. Billy sat down, keeping a wary eye on the bee. It lit on the log next to the captain, but he paid it no attention. Georgie leaned foward, waiting for the captain to resume his story. "So, you had a truce?" he asked.

"Yep, we met the Rebs on the banks of the river, and we both went swimmin'. That's when I learned thet Lieutenant Jim Chandler of the Confederate States of America—thet's what those boys called their new country—was down in the river and wanted to meet with the 'blue-belly captain who can't hit a hardball for beans.' 'Course I went down to see him." A subtle smile escaped from the captain's taut lips.

"Jim and me, we sat down in that cool mud and talked about the old days. The good days, before Fredericksburg and Gettysburg and a dozen other battles you know nothin' about. And eventually we started talking about ball.

"'Lawd, I ain't played a game in years,' Jim said. And it was then we came upon an idea. There was a clearin' between the Reb camp and the river. Normally any Yankee like me, goin' into thet field, woulda been shot dead by some Carolina boy's squirrel rifle. The same was true if a Reb had crossed the river. Except then some Ohio fella woulda done the shootin'. But thet day we had the truce, and we both agreed not to shoot anybody and to meet in the clearin' for a ball game."

"You played ball with the Rebs?" Georgie asked, scratching at the dirt with the old baseball bat. "Ain't thet against the rules or somethin'?"

"There are no rules, boys." Captain Martin tapped the bat with his cane. "Don't scar your bat up like thet. Ya gotta respect wood. It's a livin', breathin' thing, and there's somethin' magic about it."

"Just an ole messed up bat," Billy said. "It's mine, and Georgie can scuff it up all he wants."

"Corporal, back on thet river in Virginnie, we woulda given a month's pay for an old beat-up baseball bat. See, we wanted to play ball, but we didn't have the stuff. But Jim, he was nothin' if he wasn't an inventive cuss. He took a round river rock, 'bout the size of a ball, and tied some tent canvas around it with twine. Then we took some sorta straight branches and lashed 'em together to make a bat.

"It wasn't much of a game, but everybody had a great day. Jim threw stuff that everyone could hit, 'cause he knew thet's what everyone wanted to do. They wanted to wail on that ball, to take out all their misery and hate on it. They wanted to knock it to the moon. 'Course, no matter how hard you hit thet rock, it wouldn't go far."

"Who won?" Georgie asked, holding Billy's bat across his legs.

"We didn't keep score. We played the whole day, then the sun went down, and we went back to our camps."

"C'mon, mister," Billy whined. "Tell us about the fightin' and the brave stuff."

"The brave stuff, huh. Well, son, I don't know nothin' about thet. All I know is the mean stuff."

"Where's Jim at now?" Georgie asked.

The old man bit his bottom lip and scuffled some dirt with his right shoe. "About two weeks later I saw Jim again. It was rainin' somethin' awful. We could barely see thet ugly damned river. The Rebs musta known thet, 'cause they came over thet mornin'. Not much of a battle, not anything you'll ever find in a book, but Jim's boys hit us hard just before dawn.

"They came into our camp runnin' and slashin' with bayonets and swords and shootin' and hollerin'. Those Rebs could holler like devils. And they caught us by surprise. It was bad. My sergeant grabbed our flag and waved it, trying to rally our troops, and a Reb came chargin' at him out of the fog and smoke. Thet Reb had a saber—a big pigstickin' knife—held high and ready to cut my sergeant in two. His eyes were all mean, and his hair hung stringy and wet. He was the scariest thing I ever saw, and he cut down my sergeant with one swipe of thet pigsticker and turned on me. I aimed my pistol right at the Reb's head and pulled the trigger, but it didn't fire. The primer was wet.

"I thought I was dead. I panicked and just kept cockin' thet pistol and pullin' the trigger again and again, and it wouldn't fire. Thet Reb come rushin' at me with that pigsticker of his. And I don't know, maybe thet pistol's cylinder spun onto a dry cartridge, but it fired. I shot twice right into thet Reb's chest just as he started to slash at me with his knife. I got a good look at the Reb as he fell to the mud. It was Jim."

"You killed Jim?" Georgie gasped.

"But he was tryin' to kill the captain!" Billy said, defending the old man.

"Boys, I don't think Jim saw me anymore'n I saw him. There was nothin' personal in it. Combat is all noise and confusion. You don't have a lot of time to think."

Captain Martin swallowed hard, rubbed the bridge of his nose, and squeezed his eyes shut. "There are many things that make a man want to cry, boys. But there ain't nothin' worse than the death of a friend."

The boys stared at one another, then at the ground. Captain Martin stood up. "Thet's 'bout all I have to say. Many a good man died that day, and I killed some of 'em. Thet's a terrible thing, boys, to kill a man. And I never wanted to do it."

Captain Martin grabbed his cane, got up slowly, and started to walk away.

"Captain, I don't want to be in the Army to shoot no friends, just the enemy and stuff," Billy said.

"Son, you still don't understand. All the men I killed in that war . . . they may've been the best fellas there is. They mighta been daddies to good boys like you, or they mighta been murderin' scum. They coulda been farmers or teachers or doctors. They mighta even been great ballplayers. But I killed 'em 'cause somebody decided they was the enemy, and we ain't ever gonna know what they mighta been."

Georgie got up and dusted the dirt and the pine needles off the legs of his pants. "Thanks for the story, Captain."

Without a word, Captain Martin walked into the woods toward the old church and disappeared.

Billy reached under the fallen tree and pulled out something in his right hand. "Hey, mister, look at this." He held out a slightly worn baseball. "Hey, mister," he yelled after the old man, "I found one of them balls you was talkin' about!"

"I don't think he heard ya," Georgie said. "He's probably clear on the other side of the woods now."

Billy studied the ball. The leather was dried up and the seams were scuffed, but it was a real baseball. He rubbed it with his right hand, and the leather felt warm. "Want me to throw you some?"

Georgie picked up the bat.

The two boys walked to the other side of the clearing. Billy started to step off the distance between where Georgie would bat and he would throw. "How far away should I get?"

"How should I know?" Georgie asked. "Teacher never lets us play ball with them other kids."

Billy took big steps away from Georgie. "That's about thirty feet. Sound right?"

"Yeah, it'll do."

Billy lobbed the ball overhand toward Georgie like he'd seen the ballplayers do. Georgie swung hard and missed. He picked up the ball and tossed it back to Billy. "Try me again."

Billy lobbed another pitch. Georgie swung hard and smacked the ball high over the woods toward the church.

"Great, now we gotta go find it," Billy said. "This is a stupid game."

"Nah, it isn't. Thet was fun. I ain't never felt nothin' like it before. You gotta try it."

Excitedly they stomped off into the woods searching for the ball, which had come to rest behind a rusted old gate near a row of weathered granite tombstones.

"I'm not goin' in there."

Georgie put his hands on his hips, exasperated at his friend's stubbornness. "How you gonna be such a brave Injun fighter if you can't walk in a boneyard?"

"Don't wanna fight Injuns no more. Don't wanna fight nobody."

"Well, thet's fine with me, but I wanna hit again. So c'mon, let's go get our ball."

While Billy stayed put, Georgie opened the rusty gate and gingerly stepped over to the second row of gravestones.

The baseball had come to rest against the last stone in the second row. Georgie went to pick it up, then he saw the engraving on the stone:

CAPTAIN JOSIAH MARTIN U.S. ARMY
BORN DECEMBER 21, 1840. DIED NOVEMBER 2, 1863.

Georgie took a step back. His eyes darted around the cemetery. *Is it possible?* he thought. For a moment he thought of calling Billy over to look at the stone, but then he thought better of it. His friend was scared enough already. Georgie nodded at the stone to pay his respects, walked out holding the ball, and said nothing to Billy.

As they walked back to the clearing, Billy chatted about the captain's story. "You know somethin', he never told us who won thet battle," Billy said.

Yeah, he did, Georgie thought. "C'mon, let's hit."

Two young men, one in a gray Confederate officer's uniform and the other in a Union bluecoat, stood in the mists at the edge of the woods. "You see thet, Joe? Thet big kid tore the cover off'n the ball."

"Yeah, you was right, Jimmy. Thet boy's gonna be a good one. Bet he could hit even you."

"When I was on, nobody could hit me, specially not the likes of you."

"I never wanted to show you up."

Jim laughed. "Where to now?"

"New York, 1927."

The old Civil War soldiers stood in the bleachers at Yankee Stadium. It was a bright fall day, and the Yankees were playing the Tigers. The public address system boomed to life. "Now batting for the New York Yankees, Babe Ruth." The crowd erupted with cheers.

"Babe, what a stupid nickname," Jim said.

"Shut up. I wanna see this."

"What's he doing? I think he's pointing out here, Joe. He's pointing the bat out here."

Captain Josiah Martin shifted in his chair. "Stop yelling," he said, "and watch Georgie hit."

Confidence Game

The Crenshaw Oil refinery loomed on the horizon, spring sun reflecting off the silvery skin of its long metal pipes. No breeze blew across the field, and a dense smell of raw petroleum hung nasty and sweet in the warm and smoggy air.

Roberto hated playing at this field. He hated its smells, the ugly industrial sights and sounds that surrounded it, and most of all he hated playing the Crenshaw Wildcats.

From T-ball up, Crenshaw had always beaten Bobby's team, now the Gardena Giants, for the league championship. The Wildcats played on a field provided by the Crenshaw Oil Company. They had professional quality uniforms and rabid fans, who always reminded opponents how much better their team was. But none of these reasons was the root of Roberto's hate for the Wildcats.

What Bobby really hated about the Wildcats was the boy standing on the pitcher's mound, grinning in at his latest victim. The pigeon with the bat was Tommy Chun, who was facing an 0—2 count against the nastiest 14-year-old pitcher in Los Angeles County.

His name was Chuck Hansen—big for his age, tall and rangy, and all arm. All right arm. Hansen threw a sidearm fastball that should have been illegal. That pitch seemed to come right at the head of right-handed batters. Then, at the last minute, it would dart down over the plate. Tommy Chun didn't have a chance.

"Steerike!" the umpire called. Tommy walked sheepishly away from the plate and disappeared into the gloom of the Giants' dugout.

Roberto left the on-deck circle and took his position in the batter's box. Hansen grinned in. Roberto's team was down five runs in the top of the seventh inning, two out, and nobody on. The game was over. Hansen knew it, Roberto knew it, the crowd knew it. The only one in the whole park who didn't know it was Roberto's coach.

Coach Kim stood next to the dugout urging his team to give Roberto some support. "C'mon, Bobby. Pitcher's tired. Time to show him what you've got. You're the man, Bobby. You're the man."

Bobby scuffed the dirt in front of the plate with his cleats, spit out the shell of a sunflower seed, and squinted at Hansen.

Hansen wound up and delivered. Bobby didn't even move the bat off his shoulder. He heard the ball hit the catcher's mitt. He never saw it.

The Wildcats' catcher taunted Bobby. "Hey, Nunez. Why don't you go sit down. I'll catch two more, and we'll call it a day. What d'ya say?"

Bobby stepped out of the box and took a practice swing.

Crenshaw's shortstop laughed. "Look at that," the freckle-faced kid yelled. "He's got four eyes and can't see the ball with any of 'em."

Bobby got angry. He wasn't used to having people make fun of him, especially not on a baseball field, where he had always been a standout player, always been the kind of hitter that the other team feared.

"Shake it off, Bobby. Don't let 'em rattle you," Coach Kim yelled.

Bobby spit in front of the plate. Hansen wound up and fired. Bobby saw the pitch leave Hansen's hand, and he tracked it to the plate. It was right down the middle. He swung hard. He was going to crush the ball and knock the laughing shortstop on his butt.

He missed.

The next pitch was in the dirt. Bobby swung anyway.

Game over.

Coach Kim stood next to the dugout with his hands on his hips. The Wildcats didn't bother celebrating their victory. They expected to win. It was routine. Coach Kim directed his team back on the field for the "good game" high-five with the other team. Hansen stood next to the mound, smiling smugly. The grinning shortstop stood next to him. "Hey, Bobby, you're the man," Hansen said.

"Maybe you need bigger glasses," the shortstop added.

Bobby walked off the field. "Shake it off, kid. Everybody has bad days," Coach Kim said.

It took two bus transfers and nearly an hour for Bobby to ride to his mother's business after the game. He could almost have walked there in that time. Finally the bus pulled up next to a small strip mall. Bobby got off and walked from the bus stop across the parking lot toward a small drugstore. He opened the door and went inside.

His mom was behind the counter at the back of the store, working on a prescription for an elderly woman who sat on a bench in front of a rack of pamphlets about how to cope with arthritis, hypertension, and a dozen other ailments. Bobby's mom smiled up at him from behind her thick glasses and went about her work.

"Mrs. Goldstein, I'd like you to meet the best hitter in the South Bay Babe Ruth Leagues: my son, Roberto."

"Nice to meet you, young man," the old woman said. "Your mom sure is proud of you."

Mrs. Goldstein was right. Bobby's mom *was* proud of him. There were pictures of him under the glass counter, on the walls behind her, even on the cash register. The photos showed Bobby playing ball, swimming, holding the trophy he'd won last year for the highest batting average in the South Bay Little Leagues, and beside them was his report card—not straight As, just As and Bs, but Mom was proud of it anyway.

All of those pictures seemed to mock Bobby. They were shots of a boy who didn't wear glasses. None of them was of the loser he had become last month when one of his mom's doctor friends discovered Bobby was nearsighted and put the black plastic frames and thick acrylic lenses on his face. "Here you go, son. Funny thing, you're going to discover trees aren't big green blobs," the doctor had said when he fit the glasses to Bobby's face.

The doctor had been right. Bobby discovered that a lot of things looked different than he thought. He'd also discovered that baseballs didn't look as big to him anymore.

Bobby's mom handed Mrs. Goldstein her medicine, and the old woman turned to Bobby. "Nice meeting you,

Roberto. You certainly are a fine young man." Bobby didn't say anything, and Mrs. Goldstein walked away.

"Roberto Nunez. You were rude to her," Bobby's mom chided. "You know I depend on my customers. You have to be nice to them, because they can go to other stores. Do you understand?"

"Sorry, Mom."

Mom gazed thoughtfully into Bobby's face. "How'd the game go?"

"We lost."

"Well, you'll get them next time," she said with a smile.

The next few weeks passed very slowly. There were six games. The Gardena Giants only won one of them; worse, Bobby struck out so many times that he couldn't remember them all, and twice with the bases loaded. In more than thirty-six at bats, Bobby had one hit and two walks. In all, he'd only been on base three times in six games. Last year in the same number of games he would have been on base more than twenty times.

To anyone else, the reason for Bobby's slump would have been clear. The pitchers in Babe Ruth League were bigger and stronger than the ones in Little League. But Bobby had never had this bad a batting slump. He'd always been a slugger, all the way back to T-ball, and the only thing that could explain it in his mind was the glasses.

Bobby hated his glasses. Each day, he took them off on the bus, but when he got to school he couldn't read the chalkboards without them, and he had to put them on.

Some of his classmates made fun of him. And the girls looked at him like he was a nerd. It might not have been so bad if he had better looking frames. A lot of seventh-grade guys had glasses at Gardena Junior High, but Bobby had cheap glasses. He had the $50 Lenscrafters® specials with the thick black frames and thick acrylic lenses. He tried to get his mom to buy him another pair with cool metal frames and thinner lenses like the ones Steve Polonia had, but frames like Steve's cost $200, and there was no way Mom could afford that. Nobody ever called Steve "four-eyes."

Last year Bobby's teammates had nicknamed him "Blaster," because he launched so many homers. Now, he was the loser in the cheap glasses who couldn't hit.

But Coach Kim stood by Bobby throughout his slump. Even when other boys on the team started to talk about Bobby behind his back, the coach was there trying to keep his spirits up. He took the whole team to the batting cages at Baseball City, but he spent extra time with Bobby. When Bobby failed to hit slow pitches from the pitching machines, Coach Kim said his timing was off. He tried to show Bobby what he needed to do on the high-speed pitching machine nicknamed "Nolan Ryan." Bobby kept insisting he couldn't see the ball because of his glasses, but when he took his glasses off, he couldn't hit the slow machines, much less the fast ones.

The bell at the top of the door frame jingled, and Bobby's mom looked up from the prescription she was filling. "Oh, good morning, Coach. I'll be with you in a moment."

"No rush, Mrs. Nunez. I only wanted to talk for a moment."

Bobby's mom finished filling the prescription order and dropped it in a box marked "F" on the back shelf. When she turned back around, she said, "What did you want to talk about, Coach?"

"Perhaps we should talk somewhere else."

"It's difficult for me to leave the store, Coach."

"You must be a very busy woman, Mrs. Nunez."

"You don't know how busy, Coach. When I went to pharmacy school, I never dreamed of owning my own store. This was all Jorge's idea. I wish he was here to help. I can't afford to hire another pharmacist so I have to do all the work. It's really tough. Sometimes I get so angry at Jorge for leaving me like this, but . . ."

Coach Kim looked puzzled.

"My husband was killed in a car accident three years ago. It's been tough on Bobby, and on me. But this store was Jorge's dream, so when the money came from the insurance company, I bought it. That's why I haven't been to many of Bobby's games this year. Isn't that why you're here, Coach?"

"I didn't come here to get you out to the games," Coach Kim said. "Mrs. Nunez, your son has tremendous potential as a ballplayer. He's the reason I decided to coach Babe Ruth League this year instead of staying with the Little League kids. I knew that with the proper coaching he could be great. But this year he just seems lost."

"Lost?"

"Well, maybe lost isn't the right word. I don't know. He's just so down on himself lately that…You know last practice he asked me to take him out of the clean-up spot. That's not what a coach wants to hear from his star player. Bobby should want to play. He should want to bat clean-up because he knows he can help the team. I just don't know what's wrong with him. Do you?"

"Well, I have some idea," she said. "He's been very upset about his glasses. He claims he can't see the ball as well with them."

"Does that make any sense?" Coach Kim asked, leaning against the counter.

"No, of course not, Coach. Bobby actually sees better with his glasses. But he thinks they cause him to strike out. Just like he thinks they make him ugly. And the mind is a powerful thing."

"That's another thing, Mrs. Nunez. His attitude seems to be getting worse and worse."

She looked down at the counter for a moment. "It's not easy raising a teenage boy alone, Coach. There's so many things, drinking, drugs, gangs. I've been very thankful for baseball. It's Bobby's passion, but when things don't go well for him, he gets very down on himself. Then, well . . . I worry."

The coach rubbed his chin. "He needs to start hitting again. We play Crenshaw again on Saturday. They're the toughest team in the league. If we lose, we'll be five games back with seven to play. All we'll be able to do is play out the season, and we can beat those guys. I know we can. The boys just have to believe we can."

"That's easier said than done. Like I said, the mind is a powerful thing, Coach."

"Yes, I know, but if Bobby doesn't straighten up, I'm going to have to bench him."

"Maybe that's just what he needs," Mrs. Nunez said. "Maybe he needs you to stop being so nice. Maybe you *should* bench him."

Coach Kim thought about that for a moment. He thought about his own experience in youth baseball, and he realized that the coaches he remembered, the ones who really taught him the game, were tough. They were fair, but they were tough. "You've given me something to think about, Mrs. Nunez," the coach said.

Coach Kim threw nothing but sidearm fastballs throughout the afternoon practice. His arm felt like a numb rag hanging from his shoulder, but by the end of practice, everyone on the Gardena Giants had hit the ball hard. Everyone except Bobby.

The coach huddled the team around. "All right, boys. Good, hard work today. Take a lap and go home." As they started to fan out and run, he called out to them. "Remember, be here Saturday morning, nine-thirty. Game starts at ten. We play Crenshaw, and we don't want them winning on our field. Do we?"

"No, Coach," the team yelled in unison, following their standard post-practice drill.

Bobby had just started to run when Coach Kim pulled him aside. "Bobby, hold up a minute. We need to talk. You're still late through the zone."

"I know. I just can't see the ball that good anymore, Coach."

"Then I'm going to have to make a change."

"Huh?"

"Bobby, I like you. This isn't personal, but I'm benching you for the next game. You'll have to decide if you want to work hard enough to be on this team or if you're just going to keep doggin' it and blaming your glasses."

"Coach, I'm not doggin' it."

"Bull. A lot of great players wore glasses. So no more excuses. Either start hitting or I'm gonna have to bench you permanently."

"Cut me?"

"There's nineteen other guys on this team, and there's other guys out there who want to play. Maybe you just don't have what it takes."

Bobby felt angry tears well in his eyes.

"You gonna stand here or are you gonna hustle?" the coach asked, cutting his eyes toward the rest of Bobby's teammates.

Bobby took off running. His mind reeled as Coach Kim's words rang in his ears. *Maybe you just don't have what it takes.* He fought off the urge to cry. The last thing he wanted to do was start bawling in front of his teammates.

The bus dropped Bobby two blocks from home in front of a liquor store. He walked down the street past video stores, check-cashing companies, and walls spattered with incomprehensible graffiti.

At the Jack in the Box he cut across the parking lot, into the alley, and onto a small street lined by houses and apartment buildings. He walked up the street to a small stucco bungalow house, put his key in the lock, and went inside. Mom wouldn't be home for a few more hours, so Bobby went to his bedroom and fell onto his bed face down.

He lay there motionless for a few minutes. Then he lifted his head from the pillow, rolled over, and stared up at the ceiling. Coach was benching him for Saturday's game. It was the first time in his life that Bobby wasn't going to start a baseball game. He'd even played once with the flu, even after his mom told him he couldn't. Now, through no fault of his own, just because he couldn't see the ball as well as he used to, he was going to be benched. It wasn't fair.

Maybe you just don't have what it takes.

It wasn't fair.

When his mom came home about an hour later, Bobby was still staring at the ceiling and moping. She knocked on his closed door. "'Berto. You OK?"

Bobby didn't answer.

She opened the door and found Bobby lying on the bed staring up at the ceiling. "'Berto, is something wrong?" Her forehead furrowed with worry wrinkles.

"No. I'm OK." The last thing he wanted to do was tell his mom he was being benched.

"How was school?"

"All right."

"And practice? How'd you play?"

"It was all right, too, Mom. I really don't want to talk about it."

"Hey, I have some good news," she said. "I hired a temporary pharmacist today, so maybe I can break away a few hours this weekend and come to the game."

Bobby felt his heart sink. *Great,* he thought. *Mom comes to one game all year, and it's the one where I have to ride the bench.*

He looked at his mother, forced a smile, and said, "That's great, Mom. Really."

The next day at school, Bobby spent a lot of time thinking about how he could prove to the coach that he really wanted to play. He would give anything not to ride the bench for the rematch with Crenshaw. He decided to take action.

After school, Bobby rode the bus to South Bay Shopping Mall and caught another bus to Rolling Hills Mall. He was only ten miles from home, but it seemed like another world. There were big houses overlooking the ocean. Fast, expensive cars. Swimming pools. Horse stables. The only reason the buses came up here at all was to bring the poor women up to the big houses on the Palos Verdes cliffs, where they worked as maids and nannies.

Coach Kim lived up here in the hills. Bobby didn't know how the coach became so wealthy. All he knew was Coach Kim was originally from Gardena, and now he lived up here. But the coach was generous with his money. He bought the team their uniforms, their equipment, paid their insurance bills and their registration fees. And every year, at the end of the season, Coach Kim invited the team up to his house for a pool party and barbecue.

Bobby walked several blocks from the mall, turned on Gillian Way, then looped back toward the ocean on Dana Drive. Halfway down the street he reached the gated driveway of Coach Kim's house. He could see the house and the Coach's Porsche through the steel bars. The house was three times the size of Bobby's but small for this neighborhood.

Bobby pushed the intercom button on the gate. A woman's voice answered. "Hello?" she said in a strong accent Bobby didn't recognize.

Bobby spoke into the intercom. "Hi, I'm Bobby Nunez. I'm here to see Coach Kim. Is he here?"

"Is he expecting you?"

"No. No, I guess not," Bobby said. "But ask him if he'll see me, please."

She didn't answer. Bobby waited, and a few minutes later the gate swung open. The woman with the accent stood on the front step. "Mr. Kim is in the pool," she said. "He asked me to escort you."

She walked into the house and Bobby followed her.

Coach Kim vaulted out of the pool just as Bobby walked onto the deck. The coach was in good shape for an older guy—nearly forty—and his skin was dark from many hours in the sun.

The pool was kidney-shaped and large, with blue ceramic tile surrounding it. A lounge chair and a table and chair set stood on the far side of the pool. One of the chairs was draped with a white robe, and a Macintosh PowerBook notebook computer was open and running on the table in front of it. Next to the computer was a metal tray, holding a plastic pitcher of cold water and a couple of glasses. Bobby could see the ocean a few miles in the distance, and it wasn't nearly as hot here as it was down in Gardena.

Coach Kim sat at the table in front of his PowerBook and motioned Bobby into a chair facing him. The coach poured two glasses of water and handed one to Bobby.

"OK. What brings you up here, Bobby?"

All day Bobby had been thinking about what he would say to Coach Kim, and now all his rehearsed words failed him. He drank his water, looked at the coach, and stammered, "I, uh...I've been thinkin' about what you said, Coach. I was wondering if...uh, you'd help me."

"Help you?"

"Yeah. I don't want to sit on the bench, Coach. Not Saturday."

The coach rubbed his eyes like a man with a headache. "Bobby, whether you sit or play Saturday is up to you."

"I don't understand."

"Part of your problem," the coach said, "is that baseball has always come easy to you, Bobby. Am I right?"

Bobby looked confused.

The coach looked past Bobby to the ocean. "When we're really good at something, we get used to it being easy." He narrowed his eyes. "Do you understand what I'm saying?"

Bobby said he did, but he didn't, and the coach could see the lack of comprehension in the boy's eyes.

"With me it was a computer language. All my life I'd been great at math and computers. Then my sophomore year at UCLA they made me learn Machine Language. That's a computer assembly language. At first I took it for granted. I'd been good at everything else with computers, I'd be good at this, too. I didn't study it any harder than any of my past courses. You know what happened?"

Bobby shrugged.

The coach leaned forward. "I failed my first test. Absolutely bombed it. That told me something." The coach didn't wait for Bobby to respond. "It told me I was going to have to work harder. See, Bobby, being good at something will only take you so far. Why do you think you're striking out so much now?"

"I can't see the ball so good, Coach."

"Why is that?" the coach asked, pouring Bobby more water.

"It was bigger without my glasses," Bobby said, unconsciously pushing his glasses back up on his nose.

"Last week you tried to hit without your glasses, and you didn't touch the ball."

"Yeah, but my timing was off."

"Your timing is off because the pitchers have gotten better than you. That's what happens when you're good at something. There's always somebody better. And the better you get, the better they get. Half the pitchers you faced in Little League last year didn't move up to Babe Ruth level. Right?"

"Yeah, so?"

"Some of 'em weren't serious enough about baseball to keep going. Some of 'em weren't old enough to move up. Others just stunk. And you ate those guys alive. But now everybody you're facing was good enough or serious enough to move up to Babe Ruth. Some of these guys, like that big blond monster we're seeing Saturday, they're older than you, they're stronger, and they were here last year. That's the challenge of coming up to the next level. You haven't been meeting that challenge. And until today, I wasn't sure you wanted to meet it."

"That's not fair, Coach. I've been practicing hard."

"Not hard enough. You want to beat guys like Hansen, you have to learn how to stand in against him. You have to be brave and proud and realize that there are no excuses. So what if you wear glasses? There've been one-armed players in the Majors. There've been tons of guys who couldn't see without glasses or contacts. There've been small guys, thin guys, slow guys. They didn't quit. They did the job. They got it done. They worked hard and they believed in themselves.

"Your call, Bobby. Are you willing to work harder than you've ever worked before?"

Bobby swallowed and nodded yes.

"Great. Go inside, call your mom and tell her where you are. Then let's go to Baseball City. I want to show you how to hit an inside fastball. But you have to do everything I tell you to do without any questions. Agreed?"

"Agreed."

They spent the next three hours at Baseball City. The coach showed Bobby how to time his swing to Hansen's pitches. He explained to Bobby that all he had to do was see where the ball was going. Hansen threw only fastballs, and if Bobby could time one of them, Gardena would score some runs.

As they left Baseball City and got in the coach's Porsche, Bobby finally asked the coach a question he'd wondered about for a long time. "Coach, is it working hard that made you so rich?"

His money wasn't something the coach like to talk about, but he decided to answer Bobby's question. "Yeah, I worked hard, Bobby. But I'll tell you something most rich people will never admit. Hard work was only part of it." He turned the ignition key, and the Porsche roared to life. "Working hard is a key to success, but it's not the only thing. My father and my mother worked harder than I'll ever work, and they never made much money."

The coach shifted the Porsche into reverse, backed out of his parking spot, shifted into first and gunned it into the street. "I made all that money 'cause of my hard work, but mostly my parents' hard work put me in position to make it. My folks came here from Korea with nothing. My parents, man, they were tough. Homework was the most important thing. The only thing my Dad let me do other than study and work was play sports. He was tough, but I appreciate it now. It's all about hard work, Bobby. Hard work and a little luck. Your mother's trying her best to give you the same opportunity. Meet the challenge, Bobby."

For the first time in months, Bobby felt determined.

The game was on Gardena's home field, a high school athletic field that fronted a rundown portion of Western Avenue. The school, its dirty stucco walls marked with the spray-painted symbols of hundreds of taggers, could be reached by a long fly ball. All around the school, there were autobody shops, check-cashing businesses, fast food stores, lunch counters, and other small businesses common in low income neighborhoods in Los Angeles county. The signs on the businesses formed a strange linguistic stew of English, Spanish, Korean, Chinese, Japanese, and Arabic.

It was smoggy at game time. The kind of smog that L.A. was famous for—a low coastal fog that drifted inland and trapped all the car emissions and smoke from fires and furnaces in a thick brown carpet of still air. The sun burned bright through the haze, bleaching the color out of the day.

Gardena was down 2 to 0 in the bottom of the first inning. Their pitcher, Brian Foster, had walked the first two Crenshaw batters, thrown a wild pitch, and surrendered a double to Chuck Hansen. That shot had screamed down the right field line, and if Bobby hadn't played it perfectly and hit his cut-off man, the score would have been 3 to 0. Bobby's fielding inspired Foster. He settled down and the next three Crenshaw batters made quick outs.

Coach Kim felt good as his team went to bat. Chuck Hansen's vicious fastballs changed that thinking very quickly. He struck out all three Giants batters.

Gardena kept the game close in the second. Foster struck out two, gave up a solo home run, and Bobby made a diving catch of a weak line drive.

Coach Kim punched the air with enthusiasm. "Great catch, Bobby," he said as Bobby came into the dugout. Then he pulled Bobby aside to talk to him. "Bobby, we need you. You hit the Nolan Ryan machine at Baseball City. That's eighty-five mph. You can hit this guy. I know it, and you know it. Just go up there and do it."

Bobby picked his favorite bat, the blue one with the aluminum worn at the sweet spot, and went to the plate.

"Batter up!" the umpire called.

"Easy out. Blind batter. Blind batter," the Wildcats' freckle-faced shortstop yelled.

Bobby stepped into the batter's box and stared grimly out at the grinning face of Chuck Hansen. The pitcher wound up, his long, right arm snaked out toward third base, and a fastball sailed over the inside corner of the plate for a strike. Bobby watched it all the way to the catcher's glove. "That's the best look you're gonna get all day," the Wildcats' catcher said to Bobby.

Bobby didn't reply.

Mrs. Nunez was standing next to Coach Kim, talking to him through the wire fence dividing the stands from the field. "What's he doing? That was a strike. Shouldn't he have swung?"

"He's doing exactly what he needs to do. He's timing

39

this kid." The coach yelled out to Bobby, "All right, Bobby, he's yours."

Hansen's next pitch was off the outside corner and low.

"Good eye, Bobby, good eye," Coach Kim called.

The next pitch was up and in. Bobby backed out of the box. The shortstop laughed and Hansen grinned.

He's gotta come back in now, Bobby thought. Hansen released the ball. Bobby tracked it out of the pitcher's hand and slapped it down the third base line.

Foul.

On the next pitch Bobby lined out—a frozen rope—to the center fielder. He was running hard to first when he was called "Out."

Bobby went back to the dugout, where Coach Kim was waiting for him. "You hit the ball hard, Bobby. You'll get him next time."

The rest of the team saw that Bobby had hit Hansen, and they responded. Gardena scored two runs in the inning. Then after Al Luster, the Gardena catcher, flied out for the last out of the inning, Hansen came off the mound swearing.

"This is great," Coach Kim said to Bobby's mom as Gardena took the field for the top of the third inning.

The game stayed tight heading into the bottom of the last inning. Crenshaw was leading 6 to 4 and Bobby had two hits, a walk, and a long fly out.

Tommy Chun led off for Gardena and popped out to third. Chip Adams singled, Marv Johnson walked, and Greg Roncalli hit a routine grounder to the shortstop. It should have been a double play and the end of the game, but the shortstop was slow getting to the ball and got only one out.

Bobby came up to bat with Chip on third and Greg on first. The shortstop wasn't laughing anymore. Crenshaw's coach went to the mound to talk to Hansen.

Coach Kim called Bobby back to the bench. "You gotta be aggressive in this at bat, Bobby. They don't want to put the winning run on base, but if you take him too deep in the count, he'll walk you, and Brian hasn't had a hit all day." The coach nodded to the Gardena pitcher who was taking hard practice swings in the on-deck circle, then turned back to Bobby. "Don't swing at garbage, but if he gives you a good one, take him deep."

Bobby stood in the on-deck circle. He took off his glasses and saw the lenses were dusted with infield dirt. *If I have to wear these things, they might as well be clean,* he thought. He pulled a white handkerchief out of his pocket and wiped the lenses.

"Batter up!" the umpire called as the meetings broke up.

Bobby put his glasses back on, dug into the batter's box, and waited for Hansen. The pitcher was rubbing the baseball in his right hand, thinking about what he had to do. He looked worried and tired, and to Bobby, it seemed like he was rubbing the baseball like Aladdin's lamp, trying to summon a magic genie to get him out of trouble.

The first pitch was high and tight. Bobby backed out of the box and fell down.

The umpire cautioned Hansen and his coach. Hansen toed the pitching rubber and looked in at Bobby. *It's coming right down the middle,* Bobby thought.

Hansen wound up and sidearmed his best fastball right down the pipe. Bobby swung and missed. Hansen was grinning again. He thought he had Bobby's number.

Coach Kim saw the arrogance returning to Hansen's face. "That's right, kid. Go to that well again," Coach Kim said, staring out at the lanky hurler.

He's coming right back down the middle, Bobby thought. *But I know I can beat him.* He visualized himself sending Hansen's next pitch screaming into the morning sunlight. For the first time in a long time, he believed in himself, believed in his ability.

Hansen came back with the fastball. Bobby swung smoothly and fast. The bat head sliced through the strike zone, the ball hit right on the sweet spot, and there was a solid clink of aluminum. Bobby ran hard down the first base line, and as he reached first, he saw the ball smack off the top of the outfield fence and roll back into right center field.

Two runs scored by the time Bobby reached second and the center fielder had just caught up with the ball. Coach Kim was in the third base coaching box pinwheeling his right arm. Bobby tapped the second base bag with his cleats and dug hard for third.

The throw came into the cutoff man, the laughing shortstop, just as Bobby reached third. He caught the ball about 30 feet behind second base on the third base side. Bobby rounded third.

Coach Kim looked out at the shortstop and waved Bobby home. "Let's see how good your arm is," the coach yelled.

Bobby tore for the plate. The shortstop's throw was a one-hopper, but it bounced a little to the first base side of the plate. Bobby was just feet away away from the plate. The catcher had the ball, but he was out of position. He would have to shift his body to tag Bobby, and he had no time to brace for the collision. Bobby hit him hard, knocking the ball out of his glove. The catcher went down and Bobby tumbled over him.

Bobby lay sprawled on the dirt next to the catcher, looking up at the umpire. The ball came to a rest five feet away from the catcher's glove, but the umpire hadn't made a call.

Coach Kim was yelling something, but Bobby couldn't understand what. He looked at his teammates in the dugout yelling and pointing toward home plate. Then he realized what was happening. He hadn't touched the base.

He staggered to his feet, went to the plate, and stepped squarely in the middle of it. "Safe!" the umpire called.

Bobby limped toward his dugout. His teammates were celebrating, the crowd was cheering from the small wooden bleachers. His mother was beaming, hugging everybody around her, and Coach Kim was pumping the air with his fist and high-fiving his players.

The teams went back to the field for the "good game" lineup. Bobby touched Hansen's right hand. "Good game, pitcher."

"Next time," Hansen sneered.

Bobby Nunez walked off the field toward his mom. Her smile was brighter than he had ever seen before. *The doctor was right*, he thought. *Things do seem bigger and better with my glasses.*

No-Hitter

*Two outs, nobody on, and the Astros are down to
their last out. Greg Maddux has baffled them all
night. But it's still only a one-run game. Maddux's
first pitch to Bagwell is just inside. That was
Maddux's 123rd pitch, and you've got to wonder if
he's getting tired. But Braves' manager, Bobby Cox,
is sticking with the four-time Cy Young winner.*

Brian McKee stared at the TV set with doubt in his eyes,
his hands joined at the palms as if in prayer. He lived for his
hometown team, the Houston Astros. He was twelve years
old, and ever since he'd been old enough to walk, he and
his dad had been watching the games together on TV.
Sometimes, when his dad's boss wasn't using his season tick-
ets and when Brian felt well enough, they even went to the
games together.

But tonight Brian was watching the game on TV alone.
His dad was out of town on business, his mom was staying
home with his baby sister—who had a strep throat—and Brian
was alone in his room in Ladybird Johnson Memorial Hospital.
Well, sort of alone. There was another guy in the room, an
older African-American kid, muscular and tall with closely

cropped hair. He'd moved in several hours earlier, around the time Brian turned the TV on to watch the game. He'd been silent for the first eight innings of the game, which pleased Brian, who preferred watching games without interruption.

Brian watched Jeff Bagwell call for a time-out and step out of the batter's box on the fuzzy old TV set, which was mounted high on the wall in the corner next to the window.

"The Astros'll lose. They always lose," the older boy said matter-of-factly, and went back to picking at a plate of hospital food.

The voice startled Brian at first. He glanced at the boy in the bed across the hospital room, then looked back at the TV. *What did* he *know about the Astros?* Brian thought, slightly annoyed. Brian believed in his team despite their lack of success the past few years. He needed to believe in something, and it seemed natural to him that it should be a professional baseball team.

Brian sneaked a look at the other boy. The guy was a high schooler, maybe even eighteen, and he appeared to be totally healthy. "They're gonna lose. Just watch. They always lose. Never pull for the Astros. They suck."

Shut up, Brain thought. He cut a baleful glance at the older guy and decided he didn't like him. Worse, he hated him. Brian just wanted to watch the game in peace. It had been a good day; the pain had been tolerable, and he had only felt a little sick to his stomach. And as a special bonus, one of the candy stripers had wheeled him down to the courtyard so he could get a little sun, but only for a short time, because the tender skin on his bald head might burn. It had been a good day, one of Brian's few good days, and now this guy was ruining it.

On the TV, Bagwell swung and missed.

"See, what'd I tell ya. Made him look bad on that pitch." The older kid slurped a soft drink through a straw. "The Astros suck."

"The Braves used to suck," Brian fired back.

"Yeah, but they got money. Nothin' stops a team from suckin' faster than money."

That last pitch was a strike, Skip, but it's not where Maddux wanted to throw it. It was so fat in the strike zone that Bagwell couldn't even believe it. He didn't even swing. Two-two count on Bagwell. Maddux looks in at Lopez. The wind and the pitch to Bagwell.

The crack of Bagwell's bat filled the hospital room.

Klesko gave it a look, but there was no doubt about that one. It rocketed over the left-field fence for a home run. It's a two-two ball game, folks, and the Braves have once again blown a ninth-inning lead. They really miss reliever Mark Wohlers.

"What happened to Wohlers, kid?" the African-American boy said, turning his attention to Brian.

"My name's Brian, not kid." Brian sighed and focused his attention on the TV, avoiding the other boy's eyes.

"Yeah, OK, Brian. I'm Pete. What's up with Wohlers?"

"He got hit with a line drive in his pitching hand last night. They had to send him back to Atlanta," Brian said in an exasperated tone.

"Man, that sucks."

"You a big Braves fan or something?" Brian asked.

"I ain't no Braves fan, kid," Pete said, tasting his vanilla pudding dessert and putting down his spoon in disgust. "The Braves suck. I just like Wohlers. He can throw a ball a hundred miles an hour. That's a real man. Him and that Rivera guy on the Yankees. They don't screw around. They just give ya the heat and dare you to hit it. That's the way to pitch."

Brian regretted ever having asked the question. And although he would rather have watched the game in silence, without any further smart-ass comments from his roommate, he somehow felt compelled to respond. "My dad says you should mix up pitches," he said, glancing at the other boy.

Pete's dark brown skin shone under the fluorescent lights of the room, and his eyes bore right through Brian like he wasn't there.

"Yeah, well, what does your dad know about baseball? Does he play ball for a living?"

Brian shifted the pillow behind his head. "He's a systems engineer with Haliburton."

Pete arched his eyebrows. "Punchin' keys for the oil companies here in Houston? So he ain't pitchin' no ball, then, right?"

The Braves' new pitcher, Steve Petty, delivers. The pitch is a change-up, and Montgomery hits a soft liner to Chipper Jones for the third out. At the end of nine, it's Braves two, Astros two.

"See, what'd I tell you, kid. The Astros suck. I bet the Braves win it in the twelfth. Wanna bet?"

"I don't bet," Brian said indignantly.

"Good thing, too, 'cause you'd lose."

Pete got out of his bed and walked to the hospital window. Five floors below, mercury lights gave the parking lot an orange glow, and car headlights bounced off the windows of the surrounding buildings.

The TV played a commercial for Busch beer followed by another for Skoal smokeless tobacco. "Oh, man, that stuff's nasty," Pete said, glaring at the cowboy dipping snuff on the TV. "You ever see anybody chew that stuff, kid? It's gross. Turns their teeth all brown, and they stand around spittin' that nasty juice into a cup. It's sick. Team captain made us all do it last year, and I damn near upchucked.

"Worse, you start dippin' that stuff, and there ain't no way you gonna get close to the ladies. They say it gives you cancer and stuff. That I can handle, but no ladies, that's a real problem. Ya know what I mean?"

Brian felt as though he'd had the wind knocked out of him. Pete had spoken the "C" word, and he hadn't even noticed that Brian was suffering from the disease. Brian was used to most people reacting to his sickness with sympathy. From nurses and orderlies to members of his own family, everyone seemed to feel that talking about his disease would somehow make Brian feel better. Most of the time this infuriated Brian. The last thing he wanted to talk about was his cancer.

But now Brian was angry that someone *hadn't* made note of his illness. How Pete could be so self-centered that he didn't even notice boggled Brian's mind. Just about anyone with half a brain who saw Brian would know he had cancer. He was pale, thin, and his head was bald except for small tufts of wispy red hair that somehow resisted the side effects of the treatment.

Pete just kept on talking, sometimes standing between Brian and the TV, throwing make-believe balls or doing other annoying things. Brian was sure the older boy was just talking to hear himself talk, and it was driving Brian crazy. He was tired, nauseated, and all he wanted to do was watch the game in peace. Brian even had the score sheets his dad had photocopied from an Astros' program so he could keep an official score of each game. Now, thanks to his obnoxious guest, he'd lost track, and he wasn't sure who the Braves had put in with the pitcher on the double switch in the ninth inning.

A commercial for Armor All vinyl protectant droned from the TV.

Pete stood in front of the TV, wound up, and dry fired a few pitches. "See, kid, this Petty guy, he's not getting any leg in the ball. You wanna throw the ball hard, you throw three-quarters, not overhand, and push off with them legs. I learned that watching old tapes of Nolan Ryan. Half fair pitcher for a white boy."

As Pete dry fired pitches, the back of his light blue hospital gown flew open. He stopped midpitch and turned toward Brian. "Hey, kid, stop lookin' at my butt."

Brian was infuriated, his face a deep shade of red. A bit of a grin crossed Pete's face.

Petty has just walked the leadoff hitter, Bell, and you know Bobby Cox didn't want the rookie to do that. The one-and-one to Spiers. Hit hard to the right of Lemke. Oh! What a play! A diving stop. The flip to Belliard covering second, and Spiers is out at first by two steps. It doesn't get any better than that, and Petty and the Braves just dodged a bullet. Incredible play by Lemke.

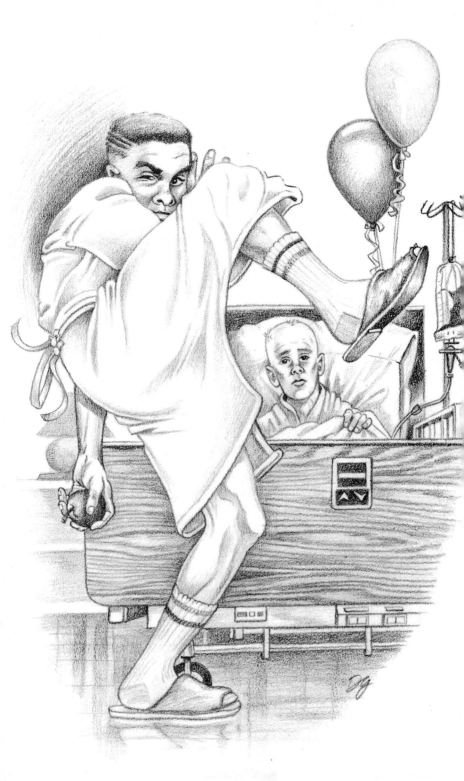

"Double play," Pete said. "Pitcher's best friend. 'Course, I don't need 'em myself."

Brian smirked. "Oh, yeah, you're so good that nobody gets on base."

"Yeah. Something like that," Pete said, sucking in his upper lip. "In less than three years I'm thirty-five and three. What do you think, kid?"

Brian snickered. "If you're so good, then I guess you've been scouted by the pros."

"Them major league scouts? Come see me? Nah, they don't spend a lot of time in little shrimpin' towns. Those boys who get scouted, they play in the cities and get their names in the papers. The only paper in my whole parish is upriver where the rich white people live."

"Not all white people are rich. I'm not rich."

Pete laughed. "Your old man's an oil engineer with Haliburton. What's he make, seventy-five, maybe a hundred Gs a year? Got yourselves a big house somewhere outside of the city here."

"We're not rich."

"Yeah. OK. So you ain't rich," Pete said, the corners of his mouth turned up in an expression of doubt. "My dad's a shrimper. He works all day out in the sun, haulin' them bugs out of the water for city people like you. So I tell you what, Brian, from where I sit you're pretty rich."

Neither boy said anything for a few minutes. Brian stared at the TV set, but he wasn't concentrating on the game. All he could think about was what Pete had said. It had never occurred to him that some people might think he was rich. Everyone he knew lived like he did, in a house in the suburbs, with a mom and dad who both worked at good jobs and drove German sedans or Volvo station wagons.

Astros closer Todd Jones has just dominated the Braves since coming on in the top of the ninth. His next test is first baseman Fred McGriff. First pitch…There's a long fly ball into right field. If it's fair, it's gone. Just foul. McGriff just missed a home run.

"A loud strike," Pete said, sitting back down on his bed. He seemed restless, and Brian could sense he was uneasy about something.

"So how fast can you throw?" Brian asked.

Pete picked up a green apple off his food tray and started flipping it absentmindedly in the air. He had the biggest hands Brian had ever seen.

"Coach brought a radar gun to practice one day, and I clocked eighty-seven miles per hour. That's real good for a high school kid," Pete said, flipping the apple. "Hell, I didn't even feel good that day. The plate felt like it was far away and stuff. If you ever pitched, you'd know what I was talkin' about."

Brian sat up in his bed. "I pitched a couple of times back in Little League," he said softly.

"If you're a pitcher, then you know," Pete said. "You know what it's like out there on that hill. The whole game is yours. Everything depends on you."

Petty appears to be tiring. He's taking much more time between pitches. Cox and Braves' pitching coach, Leo Mazzone, are going to have to make a decision. With Wohlers back in Atlanta, they don't have many choices. Mazzone goes out to the mound.

"What a wimp," Pete said with contempt.

"Who?"

"That Petty guy. He can't even last three innings when his team really needs him. What do they pay that guy anyway?"

Brian shrugged. He wasn't paying much attention to the game. Something else was on his mind; something that had been bothering him since the moment Pete had arrived. Finally he got up the nerve to ask the question that had been eating at him all night. "Why are you here?"

Pete laughed. "That sounds funny. Sounds like a guy in jail. 'What are you in for, Charlie?'"

Brian didn't get the joke.

"I'm in here," Pete said, facing the ceiling, "'cause I pulled my nets up 'fore they was full."

After a pause, Brian said, "What does that mean?"

"See this," Pete said, turning the pages of a car magazine to the center feature on the 1997 Dodge Viper. "Ten cylinders, zero to sixty in four and a half seconds. I was gonna buy one a these with the bonus money I was gonna get from signin' with a big league club, and I was gonna get my mom a nice house. One of them big houses upriver."

"What's that got to do with nets?" Brian asked.

"I had it. I had it workin' that night," Pete said. "Them white boys from upriver, they couldn't touch me. Five innings and not a hit. Not even a walk. All I had to do was finish the game."

"I don't understand," Brian said. "You were throwing a perfect game?"

"No big thing. I done it before." Pete climbed out of his bed and began rotating his arm in wide circles. "We was playin' them upriver boys on their field. They got a daily paper there upriver, and the sports guy was up in the stands taking notes on the game. There was even a photographer on the sidelines, and I saw him take my picture a coupla times." Pete's voice faded for a moment, as if he'd momentarily lost his place.

"All I had to do was get four more outs. Those upriver boys were scared of me. I could see it in the way they stood in the batter's box. They didn't want to get too near the plate. All I had to do was keep throwing strikes."

Brian knew what it was like to stand at the plate and fear a pitcher. He loved baseball, and he'd always wanted to be a great player, but he'd never been good at it, not even before his sickness.

Hudek is really throwing bullets here in the top of the twelfth. He struck out the pinch hitter Mordecai, then Justice, and now he's got Javy Lopez in the hole zero and two. Oh! Say good night, Javy. That was a nasty breaking ball, and at the end of eleven and a half, we're still knotted at two.

"That guy ain't seen nasty breaking stuff till he's seen mine," Pete mouthed at the TV.

Brian sat up in his bed. "So'd you get your perfect game?"

"Nah. I didn't get it," Pete said, shaking his head and frowning. He looked slightly detached, as if the memory of the game was too much for him to bear. "In the top of the sixth, I still got it goin', all right," he said, the excitement returning to his voice. "I strike out that first guy on three pitches.— Wham! Bam! See ya later, Sam! But while that boy is walking away from the plate, wondering what just happened to him, the home plate umpire staggers away and throws up through his mask. He then falls down, and everybody thinks he's had a heart attack. So somebody calls an ambulance. Then, while they're loading the plate umpire into the ambulance, the guy who was umpiring the outfield starts to throw up."

Brian felt queasy. "Please," he said to Pete. "I'm taking radiation therapy, and it makes me sick all the time. Don't talk about people throwing up. OK?"

"Yeah. All right," Pete said, taken aback by Brian's comments. He lowered himself onto his bed.

Brian watched as Pete's eyes seemed to fix on him. Brian knew what Pete was thinking. He looked like he was feeling sorry for Brian and probably feeling a sense of relief that he didn't have cancer himself. Brian had seen that same look hundreds of times.

"So what happened next?" Brian asked, trying to break the awkward silence.

"Yeah," Pete said haltingly. "So we ain't got no umpires, ya know, 'cause they're on the way to the hospital with food poisoning. They drove to the game together and stopped at a barbecue joint—"

"Please. I get the picture," Brian said. "So what happened at the game?"

The older boy started to talk, but he was interrupted by an orderly who came in and took both their food trays. The orderly stopped for a moment to look at the game.

Astros are threatening here in the bottom of the twelfth. This has been a whale of a ball game. Astros have Mouton on second with nobody out, and the Braves are playing deep at the corners and tight in the middle. What the Braves need here is a strikeout.

What the Astros want to do is bunt Mouton to third and try to pick up the run on a fly ball. But Eusebio is swinging away. It's a slow roller to Chipper Jones. He fires to first for out number one. Why didn't they bunt, Don?

The orderly put Brian's tray of mostly uneaten food on his cart and wheeled it away. Brian poured himself a cup of water from the pitcher beside his bed. "So what did they do? You couldn't keep playing without an umpire."

Pete gave an exaggerated sigh. "Both coaches met for a few minutes and decided to find two guys in the stands to umpire the rest of the game. It was a close game, ya know, and I don't think those upriver folks were willing to just give it to us. Naturally the first guy they went to was my brother, Clarence. I say naturally 'cause Clay had just come off duty, and he was still on call and wearing his deputy sheriff uniform. My brother's nine years older than me. He's a former all-parish running back, a marine sergeant. Got the Silver Star for bravery in the Gulf War, and the white folks like him."

"Your brother was asked to umpire a game you were pitching?" Brian asked. "That's wild."

"Yeah."

"Man, you had it made."

Pete snickered. "Yeah, well, it didn't work out like that. Ya see, my brother is a real political type. Thinks they'll someday make him parish sheriff if he kisses up to enough people."

Brian looked puzzled. "That's not a very nice thing to say."

"Ain't nice, but it's true," Pete said, popping his knuckles one at a time. "Anyway, they got Clay to do it. I went back out to the mound, took some warm-up throws, and we started playin' again.

"My brother called my first pitch a strike, and it was. I mean I threw the heat right down Main Street." Pete made a slicing motion with the heel of his left hand over the palm of his right, like a baseball cutting across a plate. "I got the first strike on those boys early in the game, and it worked like a charm, 'cause, man, I had my fastball poppin'. But I made that same pitch again, and the batter hit it hard at my third baseman. He lined out, but that was the first time in the game that anybody got around on my fastball.

"If I was going to get the next four guys out without a hit, I knew I had to start going for the corners. So that's what I did. But my brother wouldn't *give* me the corners. Clay squeezed my strike zone. I had to come right down the middle with every pitch."

Brian sat up, tense and excited.

Pete got out of bed and stood in front of Brian as though he were a batter waiting for a pitch. "After I walked the bases loaded, their best hitter came to the plate. I tried the inside corner, but Clay called it a ball. He called the next two pitches balls, even though I know they were strikes. The next pitch I tried to put a little somethin' extra on the ball, and I threw it right down the middle of the plate, belt high. And it had nothin' on it, just sat there spinning in place almost like it was on a tee. That batter knocked the cover off it."

Pete took a swing with an imaginary bat. "Boom! Grand slam. Can you believe it? I went from no-hitting those guys to losing four to three all in the same inning. Game over."

Brian could hardly believe what he was hearing. With one pitch, Pete's life had taken a dramatic turn for the worse. At least Pete thought so. "Wow," Brian said softly. "I'm...sorry."

"Coach came out and took me out of the game after that. We lost eight to six in extra innings. I didn't even get mentioned in the newspaper story except as the guy who threw the grand slam pitch."

Both boys looked up at the TV.

You know, Skip. The sad thing about a game like this is that no matter how well both of these teams play, somebody's got to lose. One of the pitchers in this extremely hard fought game is going to give up the winning RBI. Someone will be the hero and someone will be the goat.

"The thing I don't get," Brian said, searching for the remote control to turn down the TV, "is why are you in this hospital?"

"My brother put me here," Pete said, pouring water out of the plastic pitcher into his cup. "But not like you think.

"Clay cost me my chance at the major leagues. I could pitch the rest of this year and not give up a single hit, and no one would notice anything but the game against those upriver boys. That was my ticket. That was my break, and he ruined it just to keep them rich upriver people happy." Pete sat on the edge of his bed and gazed past Brian toward the window.

"Ya know," Brian said, "you're mad about a lot of stuff. But maybe your brother wasn't just kissing up. Maybe he was just trying to be fair."

"Fair?" Pete repeated with a mix of anger and surprise. "He sure wasn't fair to me."

"But you said it yourself. You were tiring. I mean, look at this game," Brian said, motioning toward the TV. "Greg Maddux, there's nobody better, right? He got tired in the ninth. They didn't pull him, and wham! Bagwell goes yard. If Maddux gives up runs when he gets tired, maybe you just did the same. Maybe it wasn't your brother's fault."

"I wasn't that tired," Pete said, glaring at Brian.

Brian glared back. "Man, you just hate everything, you know that? Just leave me alone, all right? I just wanna watch the rest of the game and go to bed." He stabbed the remote at the TV and turned up the sound.

"Hey, who's stoppin' ya?" Pete said, lying back down with his arms folded behind his head.

Brian heard footsteps in the hall. A nurse—the pretty one named Alicea—appeared in the doorway. "How are you boys doing?" she asked as she breezed into the room. "Are the Astros losing again, Brian?"

"It's tied," Brian said, scowling at Pete. "Top of the thirteenth, two out, and the Braves have a runner on second."

"Sounds exciting, but you need your rest, Brian. I'll give you fifteen more minutes, then TV off and lights out, OK?"

The nurse gave Brian some yellow pills in a paper cup. "These will help your stomach settle down, and they're going to make you sleepy." Brian took the paper cup from the nurse as she poured him a glass of water from the pitcher on his night table.

Then she turned to Pete and smiled thoughtfully. "Your mom and dad and your sisters are downstairs in your brother's room, Peter. They want you to go down. Doctor says it's OK as long as you don't eat anything after eleven-thirty and get to sleep by midnight."

Pete got off his bed and started to walk out of the room. When he reached the doorway, he turned to face Brian. "Shoulda bet me, kid. It's the thirteenth inning, and the Astros still ain't lost yet." He turned and disappeared down the dim hallway.

A pickup truck commercial played on the TV. Alicea started to leave the room.

"Alicea?" Brian called out, catching the nurse's attention before she could leave.

"Yeah, Brian?"

"Why'd they put that guy in here with me? Shouldn't they have paired me with some kid my own age?"

She walked over to Brian's bed and sat down in the chair next to it. "Pete's going through some hard times. The doctor hoped that putting him in here with you might help cheer him up."

"What's wrong with him? Has he got cancer like me?"

"Pete? Oh, no. Pete's very healthy."

"I don't get it. You put this jerk in my room and he's healthy?"

"He's not a jerk, Brian."

"Yes, he is. You should hear the things he said about his brother."

"Brian," the nurse said, taking the boy by the hand, "Pete's brother, Clarence, is a deputy sheriff over in Luziana."

"Yeah, he told me."

"Did he tell you what happened to Clarence?"

"No, he didn't say anything about that," Brian said, shaking his head.

"His brother tried to break up a convenience store robbery last weekend. The robbers killed a customer, and they shot Pete's brother."

Brian felt a cold chill run the length of his body. "Is he OK? Is he gonna make it?"

"Well, he's far from OK, but he's probably gonna make it, thanks to Pete."

Brian looked at her feeling very confused.

"Pete's brother was shot in the side, Brian, and the bullet hit both of his kidneys. He needs a transplant or he'll die."

"I don't understand," Brian said. "What's that got to do with Pete?"

"Well, Pete and his brother have a rare tissue type. There can only be two possible donors: Pete's sister, Derinda, or Pete. Derinda and her husband are expecting a baby. So Pete volunteered."

"That's why Pete is here?"

"Yes. Now fifteen minutes more of the Astros and lights out." She patted him on the arm and got up to leave.

"Alicea?" Brian said. "Can Pete play baseball with one kidney?"

"Probably not at the professional level."

"So his dad's making him do this or something, right?"

"Nobody's making Pete do anything, Brian. His family could wait for another kidney, but Pete didn't want his brother and family to worry."

She patted Brian on the arm. "Now watch your game. And get some rest. You've got a treatment tomorrow."

Brian sat in his bed watching the ball game, but he wasn't really seeing it. The TV seemed far away. The voices of the commentators sounded like a distant hum. Brian replayed most of his discussion with Pete in his head. He pictured Pete standing in front of the TV, throwing imaginary pitches and jawing at the TV commentators. He pictured the exaggerated manner in which Pete threw his arms around whenever he made a point. And then he thought about Pete's brother, Clarence, lying on the floor of the convenience store with a bullet in his side.

He wanted to talk to Pete, assure him that everything would be OK, but that would have to wait until later.

For now Brian felt somehow rejuvenated. It was hard to explain—impossible, really. Kind of like he'd just run into an old friend whose company he'd missed terribly.

Tomorrow there'd be more treatments, more pain. But he felt ready to take on anything at the moment.

Besides, the Astros were playing again tomorrow night.

There's the pitch from McMichael. And Abreau drills it down the right-field line into the corner. That's trouble. Justice gets to the ball and fires to second. But Abreau is in with a stand-up double. Runner on second, nobody out, and a run wins the game. The Astros had this situation earlier, Skip, but they chose not to bunt the runner over. Yeah, Don, but that backfired. They're going to play station-to-station here. The next play will be a sacrifice.

The Trade

Tim McCully stepped up to the plate, and the Rocket out-fielders moved in so close they were practically standing on the bases, chatting with the infielders. It was a challenge, and Tim McCully was fairly sure he couldn't meet it. He brushed the sweaty brown hair out of his eyes and choked up on the bat.

There were two outs, the tying run on third. The pitcher eyed Tim the way a hungry lizard watches a bug. He wound up and released.

The ball slapped the catcher's mitt with a dull thump. "Steerike!"

"Don't worry," Coach Davis called from the Harkerton Hawks' dugout. "Keep your eye on the ball. Next one's yours."

The words of encouragement only made Tim more nervous. They reminded him that everyone—the Hawks, the Rockets, the fans in the stands, his own parents—was watching. His stomach turned to ice water, and his hands were so sweaty he feared he might drop the bat. *If I'm lucky,* he thought, *a fastball will knock me unconscious, and I won't wake up until Little League season is over.*

"Steerike two!"

Tim didn't even see the ball. But he did hear his teammates shifting nervously on the bench, and worse, the outfielders moved in even closer. A red bubble swelled from the pitcher's mouth. Digging one foot into the dirt around the rubber, he slurped the string of gum back into his mouth and glanced over at third base.

Tim's mind began to wander. He thought about his older brother, Dan, and how he could have saved the day. He'd probably send one over the fence to win the game. *I'd give anything to be that good,* Tim thought. He imagined smashing the ball high over the right field fence, then he would circle the bases and glare at the outfielders who had mocked him. But it was useless to think about such things. He wasn't as good as his brother. Besides, Dan was . . .

The pitcher cut loose a fastball. Tim swung, made contact, and sprinted down the line to first base. But before he reached the bag, the first baseman was already jogging in. Tim had only managed a pop out to the pitcher.

After the teams shook hands, and the cheering visitors pulled away in their bus, the Hawks milled around the dugout. Nobody gave Tim a hard time. In fact, nobody said much of anything to him. They weren't ignoring him as much as tolerating him, and that felt worse. Finally Gord Foster, the Hawks' pitcher, spoke to him. "We're going to Lloyd's for sodas. You interested?"

Tim shrugged. "Nah, I'm not really in the mood. I have to get home. Thanks."

But Tim didn't go home. He slumped against the backstop, mitt between his sneakers, and stared at his baseball cap on the grass before him. The Hawks' navy blue cap was faded by the sun, the worn bill curved to perfection. The

hat used to be Dan's. Tim preferred it to his own. A few feet away bees buzzed around a trash can, and a melting rocket pop bled a red puddle in the dirt.

Dan McCully died on a rainy day the year before. He was riding his bike home after a game when he lost control on the wet pavement. His head struck a curb. He was only 15 years old. Since then nothing had been the same; everything felt somehow off balance. In two years Tim would be the same age as Dan had been, and the following year he would surpass him. But in Tim's mind Dan would always be the older brother.

Tim wanted to quit playing ball, but he knew it would kill his mom and dad.

The hot breeze shifted, and the sickly sweet smell of the trash wafted toward Tim. He buried his head in his arms.

"Tough game, son. Wouldn't blame a boy for quitting after something like that."

Tim nearly jumped out of his shirt. The voice seemed to have come from the dugout. He sidled over to the top step and peered in.

"I didn't mean to startle you," a white-haired man said. He was sitting in the middle of the bench, his long legs crossed at the ankles. Tim recognized most everyone in Harkerton, but he'd never seen this man before.

"I've seen some tough moments in baseball," the man said, "and that was one of the roughest. I've also seen moments that make the diamond shine. I was in the crowd the day Babe Ruth knocked one out of the park for that sick boy. Some say he called that shot, pointed with his bat, but that never happened."

Babe Ruth, Tim thought. *But he played in the 30s and 40s.*

The stranger shook his head and smacked his lips. "People see what they want. My name's Walker. My friends call me Satch." He extended a hand, and Tim stepped down into the dugout to introduce himself. Satch's hand was cold as clay, and Tim noticed that he was dressed in strange clothes: two-tone shoes, baggy pants, and a rumpled green shirt with a wide red tie.

"You could quit playing ball, son, but it would be a shame. You're a natural, and if anyone knows talent, it's Satch Walker. I've trained some of the greats—Ty Cobb and Chick Gandil, just to name two." Satch pulled at his chin. "What do you say I coach you, give you some pointers?"

Tim's cheeks blushed. "I don't think so. Anyway, I don't have enough money for a private trainer."

Satch turned his head as if embarrassed. "Money doesn't interest me, boy. In fact, I'll give you a free tip right now, and if you don't improve by tomorrow, you'll never have to talk to me again. But if you decide you want my help, I'm sure we can work something out."

"OK. What's the tip?"

"You need to get mean, boy. I look at you and see seventy-five pounds of *please* and *thank you*. That might work at Grandma's house, but it doesn't cut it on the field. When you see that pitch coming, think of it as someone who's done you wrong. Maybe a teacher who failed you, or a teammate who laughed when you missed a catch. Maybe even your parents."

"But I like my parents."

"Of course you do. I'm just saying that you've got to reach down and pull some meanness out of yourself."

Tim was taken aback by Satch's remarks. He had expected technical advice about weight placement, or keeping his head down in the box and his eye on the ball. He wasn't sure how to respond except to say thanks.

"Don't mention it, boy. Think it over, and maybe I'll see you tomorrow." Satch excused himself and shuffled into the gray evening, whistling an old tune.

Tim didn't expect his parents to ever fully recover from the trauma of Dan's accident. It had stolen something from them, slowed them noticeably. Lines were etched around Mr. McCully's mouth, and Mrs. McCully's eyes seemed perpetually red from crying. They were just learning to shake off the cold of that terrible day when suddenly baseball season returned. It stirred up ghosts, and summoned warm memories that easily turned traitorous. So Tim appreciated his father's efforts to console him later that night.

"What could you do against that pitcher?" Mr. McCully said warmly. "The kid really had good stuff today."

A 15-14 final was anything but a pitching duel, but Tim nodded anyway. Dinner was over, and the table had been cleared, when Mrs. McCully brought out a plate of hot brownies. Win or lose, there were always brownies after the games. By the end of the season it was amazing that either of the McCully kids could even make it around the bases. "It's not the 'breakfast of champions,'" Tim's mother said, "but they might make you feel better."

Tim forced a smile and grabbed a brownie from the plate. The first bite was pure heaven. Maybe losing wasn't so bad.

"You have to put it behind you, son," Mr. McCully said. "I remember once Dan blew a double play in a big game, and the Hawks lost. I didn't think he'd ever get over it."

"I don't mind if we give Dan credit for everything good in the world, but at least leave me the losses. I'd like credit for something." Tim didn't know why he said it. The words just leaped out like heat lightning on a quiet summer night and left only humid silence.

Before going to bed, Tim paused outside the closed door to Dan's room. The worst part about the accident was that there was no one to blame. It was a freak occurrence, a conspiracy between wet pavement and a sharp turn. Such a stupid thing, in fact, that sometimes Tim convinced himself it never happened and that Dan would just come home one day. Maybe that's why Mrs. McCully still changed the sheets on his bed and kept the room like a museum. Dan's trophies, sports magazines, and posters were all waiting where he left them. There was no one to blame. But sometimes— silently—Tim blamed Dan. He should have worn a helmet.

He shouldn't have been so good.

At practice the next day, Tim stepped into the batter's box and watched the outfielders creep forward.

"Don't mind them, Timmy boy. Head down. Keep your eye on the ball." Coach Davis's voice grated on Tim. It was playful and over supportive, like he was coaching a five-year-old playing T-ball for the first time. It made him even madder that Gord's first pitch was soft. Tim caught it with a bare hand and tossed it back. "Give me your best stuff," he snarled. He could hardly believe his own words.

Gord did, and Tim clobbered it. The outfielders just stood there, slack-jawed, watching the ball sail high and drop into the parking lot beyond the right-field fence. It was a perfect enactment of what Tim had imagined at the plate the day before.

"Nice," Coach Davis croaked, his voice colorless with shock. He pulled a ball from the bucket at his feet and tossed it out to Gord. "Try again."

The next pitch landed five feet from the first one. A grim smile of satisfaction bent Tim's lips as the outfielders marched to their true positions.

Coach Davis kept Tim swinging for nearly 20 minutes. *Doesn't he believe it's possible for me to be this good?* Tim thought. *Well, I'll show him!* Gord couldn't get anything past him. Tim's bat caught every pitch with the crack of a rifle shot, and each swat was more fierce than the last. Tim's jaws clamped so tightly with determination that he thought his teeth might shatter.

Finally the bucket was empty, and Coach Davis sent the team out to retrieve the scattered balls. He stared at Tim like a man who had just discovered gold coins in a wastebasket. "Why don't you take a rest." He was already scribbling a new batting order for tomorrow's game against the Barryville Broncos as Tim went to the cooler.

Gord came up behind Tim and slapped him on the shoulder. "That was amazing! I've never seen anyone hit like that. Except maybe Canseco."

"No big deal," Tim said. "Besides, you were pitching like a monkey." He didn't look at Gord. The dense silence hanging between them was enough. It was perfect. For once Gord had nothing to say.

Finally Gord spoke, his voice flat and cold. "Let's just see if you can hit like that in a game," he said.

"With you pitching, I'll have to."

Tim sat at the top of the bleachers and watched his teammates head home. He pulled the faded baseball cap snugly over his crown and thought, *out of the park . . . I've never done that with one ball, let alone a bucketful.* It wasn't like he had beaten the Green Monster at Fenway Park—after all, the Harkerton outfield wall was only a lazy strip of snow fence, but it sure did feel good. It felt even better to show up Gord and the others who had doubted him.

The field and neighboring playgrounds were empty now. Tim was about to leave, too, when he heard the familiar voice.

"Satisfied with the results? I'd say that was your best day ever." Satch Walker huddled next to Tim on the bleachers.

"Yeah, but I don't think it had much to do with your advice."

"How do you explain it then?" Satch's bony fingers scratched his eyes. "I saw the hate in your eyes. It felt good, right? Did you imagine the ball was the head of the pitcher, or that stupid gloating coach?"

Tim tugged at the bill of his cap. He didn't know what gloating meant, but something in his gut told him that Satch was right. Anger had risen up in him like a black gusher. It oiled his muscles and ignited his competitive spirit. "OK, maybe you had something to do with it."

Satch nodded. "And we're not done yet. Hitting is only part of the package. We've got to work on fielding. Wouldn't it be embarrassing to go to Barryville tomorrow, knock a few out of the park, and be all thumbs in the field?"

Tim's shoulders slackened and he bit his lower lip. How many times had he let a ball slip past his glove, or simply lost one because he'd flinched at an unexpected bounce? Some kids said he had hands of stone. "All right, let's go to work."

"Work is for no-talents, son. You're a natural. We've just got to get your mind right." He rubbed his weathered hands together. "First, let's talk about payment."

"Mr. Walker, you said you wouldn't charge me."

"Please, call me Satch, all my friends do."

"Satch, I told you I don't have much money." Tim heard a tremor in his voice. It would be tragic to pass up such an opportunity. "I'll give you whatever I can, but—"

"I told you I'm not interested in money, boy. I thought we could make a trade." His brow creased in contemplation, and he stroked his upper lip. "That's a fine cap. All broken in and soft. I bet it fits like a dream. I could use something like that to keep the heat off my brain."

"Satch, I couldn't. Not this hat."

"What's a hat? Does it compare to winning a championship?" Satch's eyes glistened, and his smile exposed a mouthful of greasy teeth like dirty rocks. "Think of the smiles on your parents' faces when you bring home a division trophy. Imagine the way it will shine on your shelf."

Tim pulled the cap off his head and studied it. Written on the inside band in black ink was the name Dan McCully. It was old and ragged, a little stained. It did seem a small price to pay.

"Son, the division would only be the start." Satch's hand swept across the horizon of bruised clouds and diminishing daylight. "I'll take you to the big leagues, maybe even the World Series."

Tim handed over the cap. Satch folded it once, deposited it in a wine-dark pocket, and stood swiftly. "It's been a pleasure doing business with you, son."

"What about my lesson?" Tim asked weakly.

Satch didn't even look back. "Don't worry," he explained. "You're a natural." A sly evening breeze followed him as he descended the bleachers. Tim watched a paper bag twist high in the gray air. When he looked back, Satch was gone, and Tim felt a chill crawl over him.

Harkerton trounced Barryville 8–1. The Broncos may have had the best team in the division, but they were no match for the Hawks' new secret weapon, Tim McCully. With his first swing Tim knocked the ball out of the park, then strode around the bases proudly. But when he returned to the dugout, his teammates practically ignored him. There were a few high-fives, but with the exception of Coach Davis, no one seemed to have noticed. Tim slumped at the end of the bench and stewed. It was obvious that Gord, still angry about practice yesterday, had turned the rest of the team against Tim. *What does it matter*, he thought. *They're all his friends anyway. I don't care about them.* The dark flood of anger that had been building since his first meeting with Satch was reaching a fever pitch. Tim knocked five more out of the park and drove in two other runners for good measure. Each pitch came in slow motion and seemed as large as a beach ball. Even when they tried to walk Tim, the ball somehow found his bat and went flying.

Standing around in right field irritated Tim. He made one impressive diving catch, but that was it. Gord was pitching a good game, and there wasn't much action. Tim's new cap felt foreign on his head, and he kept fidgeting with it. After a while, his scalp started itching, and the sun's glare gave him a headache. He'd have to talk to Coach Davis later. He was being wasted in this position. First base was where he belonged. Or maybe on the mound.

Satch, what do you say to pitching lessons?

On the way back to Harkerton after the game, Coach Davis insisted on taking the team for pizza. After any other game, this offer would have been met with enthusiastic cheers. But today the Hawks barely spoke, and the bus ride was strangely quiet. Coach Davis was so pleased with his brilliant coaching that he didn't notice.

"Wait until we play Potterville," Coach Davis said, yanking a stringy slice of pizza from the pie. "We'll pay them back for that loss two weeks ago."

Tim didn't eat any pizza. His one slice went cold, and the grease turned the paper plate gray. He was stuck at a table with the coach and the equipment manager, Doug Meyers, who had a cold and blew his nose nonstop. The rest of the Hawks crowded around another table laughing, shooting napkin wads through straws, and congratulating Gord on his great pitching. *I should be there,* Tim thought. *I won the game for them. The only reason Gord pitched well is because he was mad at me. Satch is right: Anger makes you good.* His head throbbed, and his stomach felt like someone had a hold of it and was twisting.

"Tim, you're going to shock those Potterville Pirates," Coach Davis said around a mouthful of cheese, a drop of grease hanging from his bottom lip. "Actually, I bet the coaches are already burning up the phone lines talking about the show my new star put on."

Tim shot the coach a venomous stare. "I'm not your star. Don't try to take credit for my talent. You didn't have anything to do with it." Tim stood suddenly, knocking over his chair, and yelled at the rest of the team. "I won that game. If it weren't for me, it would have been a one-nothing loss. Just remember that." He marched out of the restaurant.

It was after dark by the time he reached his house. When he clattered through the kitchen door, his father cheered and his mother locked her arms around him, kissing him proudly. None of this helped his headache or stomachache.

"Gord's mother called and told us," Mr. McCully said, ruffling Tim's hair. "Five runs! I should have been there."

"Actually, it was six runs," Tim said, shrugging off his mother's embrace and heading to the sink for a glass of water. He needed something to calm the pounding in his head.

"Do you feel like a champion today?" Mrs. McCully said, handing Tim a hot brownie on a paper napkin.

Mr. McCully was still shaking his head in amazement. "Six runs. I wish I had it on tape. I definitely should have been there."

"I'm sure if *Dan* was playing you would've been there," Tim snapped and grabbed another brownie from the plate.

"What's that supposed to mean?" Mr. McCully demanded.

"Sorry, I didn't mean to insult the great Dan. Why should you come to my games? It's not like you expect anything good from me. But that's going to change. From now on, no one will even remember Dan McCully."

Mr. McCully's lips pursed and his face went red. His voice was a hoarse whisper. "Go to your room."

Tim stomped upstairs, but he didn't go to his room. He went to Dan's instead and curled on the floor, pulling his knees into his stomach. The bronze trophies and dangling medals glowed warmly in the shadows.

Do you feel like a champion today?

Definitely not. Two days ago it had been his dream to play great ball and carry the Hawks to victory. Suddenly that was a reality, and instead of feeling good and celebrating, he was curled in the dark like a raw shrimp. His skull throbbed and the thought of food made his stomach crawl. His parents were angry; his teammates wanted nothing to do with him. To be honest, he didn't blame them. He didn't much like himself, either. Instead of a champ, he felt like a satellite torn from its orbit and spiraling into space.

But if Satch can make me as good as those other guys he's worked with, it's all worth it. Isn't it?

This made Tim wonder. He fumbled through the dark to find the desk lamp, turned it on, and pulled a baseball encyclopedia from the bookshelf. He turned the pages, found the names, and read the stories.

Satch had said his students were famous. *Infamous* was a better word. Chick Gandil was the Chicago first baseman who organized the World Series scandal of 1912. He convinced some of his teammates to lose the World Series for money. He was banned from the game for the rest of his life. Ty Cobb was remembered more for his drinking, gambling, and brawling than for the power of his bat. Even his teammates didn't like him. He suffered ulcers and sometimes slept with a pistol under his pillow.

Fear like wet leaves clung to Tim's spine. *Is this what Satch is really training me for?*

Then he realized the worst part—the dates! If Satch had been a coach in 1912, he would be over 100 years old today. It was impossible! "Dan," Tim whispered, "I think I'm in trouble. I know I seem resentful at times, but that's only because you were so good and left some pretty big shoes to fill. I really wish you were here to help me right now."

Tim slipped into a thin, dreamless sleep. When he woke, his head was clear and his stomach calm, and he knew what he had to do. He grabbed a Louisville Slugger from the corner and snuck out of the house with his glove and a ball. Even though it was nearly midnight and a full moon hung in the sky like a leering skull, Tim knew he would find Satch Walker at the baseball field.

The lights were on at the field, burning far brighter than normal. They cast wild, harsh shadows like spilled oil that bleached the base paths as white as bone. Satch was draped in black sweats, the hood of his sweatshirt pulled over his head. He waited against the backstop like a spider in a web.

"I thought you might come down tonight." Satch's tone was one of amusement, but there was no warmth or humor in his voice.

"I have some questions."

"They usually do," Satch muttered under his breath. "Tell me what concerns you."

Tim wasn't sure how to say it. The thoughts were so crazy, they couldn't be harnessed by words. Finally they just jumped out. "I think you're the Devil, and you want to take my soul."

Satch chuckled like a hissing radiator. "How do you know I don't have it already?" he said, grinning. "In truth, your soul is neither mine to take nor yours to give. I have other interests, such as . . . obedience."

"Well, you have the wrong kid."

"You can't back out now, boy. People won't let you. The word is out. Your parents will keep pushing you. Soon there will be agents with contracts and big money. You'll be a superstar."

"It's not true. You don't make champs. I know about the people you coached. They ended up disgraced."

Satch's eyes flashed a leprous gold, and he pointed a hooked claw at Tim. "I won't let you go. You're in whether you like it or not."

"How about a bet?" There was a pause—only a second—but Tim knew Satch was hooked.

"What do you have in mind?"

"An inning of baseball. First you pitch to me, then I pitch to you. One out each. Whoever hits more balls over the wall wins."

Satch smiled, revealing yellowed canines. "When I win, you'll sign a contract and play the game my way for the rest of your miserable life. And I promise, it will be miserable."

Tim felt all the blood rush out of his legs. He did his best to steady himself. "I'm going to win, and you will walk away and never come near me again. And you'll give back my baseball cap."

Satch pushed up his sleeves. The muscles of his forearms were like snakes wrapped around bones. He pulled back the hood, and his hair spilled over his shoulders in greasy coils. "Let's play." He pulled Tim's faded cap from the black pouch of his sweatshirt, hung it on the backstop, and strode out to the mound. Tim was about to toss a baseball to him when he realized Satch already had a white bucket of balls at his foot.

"I came prepared," Satch said.

This sent a chill through Tim. Satch had been ready and waiting. *I was foolish to think I could beat this guy. He's going to eat me alive. Maybe literally. Stop that! He wants you scared. Fear and desperation make him strong.* Tim stepped into the box and readied his bat. He didn't even see the first two pitches. They were blistering fastballs that nearly ripped through the backstop.

"Want to change your mind?" Satch asked.

"No way," Tim shouted back, but the nervous burn in his belly told him he wasn't as sure as he sounded.

Concentrate. Concentrate.

The next ball caught the meat of the bat and sailed into the dark. It landed beyond the fence. Tim could hardly believe his luck.

"That was a gift."

The next one went over the fence, too.

"Was that a gift, too?"

"Not bad. Did you imagine it was my head?" Satch's talons selected another ball. "Tell me who you see this time."

Tim watched the windup and release. He saw the ball sail toward him in slow motion, but just as he was about to lay into it, he could have sworn he saw a face between the laces, eyes filled with terror, mouth stretched in a silent scream. Tim screamed, and the bat slid from his hands. The next two strikes were so fast Tim barely saw them.

Satch was at his side like an icy wind. "Two over the wall—not bad, but not enough to stop me. Your turn to pitch."

Tim took the mound and brushed the dust off the pitcher's rubber with his toe. His eyes were toying with him. The distance between himself and Satch seemed to swell and shrink. Was it a mile or just the length of a bat? Tim didn't know if Satch was playing another trick or if he was falling into madness on his own. *Calm down! It's 46 feet to the plate, and you know it.* He pulled his palms across his pants to dry off the sweat and reached for a ball. To his horror, he saw that they were not in a bucket. It was the empty cradle of an upside-down skull. Tim mustered his nerves and took a ball.

He wound up.

Satch sent the ball screaming. Tim watched it vanish into the night sky and then return to Earth a sizzling meteor, sparks and blue flame spitting behind it.

The skull's empty sockets watched Tim without passion as he retrieved another ball.

Satch tied the competition with the next swat. "You know I'll win," he hissed, taking a practice swing.

Tim drew in a deep breath and released it slowly as he selected a baseball. He held it gently, searching the stitched skin for the perfect grasp.

This is it.

He let it fly.

With a crack like a snapping bone, Satch sent the ball into the night. Tim couldn't bring himself to watch. He stared blankly at his sneakers, and Satch's sour laugh filled his ears. *It's all over.*

There was another sound—the warm smack of a baseball hitting an old mitt.

Tim spun excitedly, his heart pounding his ribs. A lean, familiar outfielder stood by the snow fence. He held up the life-saving out triumphantly.

"Dan?" Tim whispered.

He watched in amazement as his brother took a few lazy steps toward the infield, gave a warm smile, and then threw the ball back to him. Tim wanted to speak to Dan, wanted to tell him how much he missed him and how difficult things had been since he left. But before he could get the words out of his mouth, his brother's image began to fade into the night, until all that remained was a hazy outline glowing in Tim's brain.

Then he remembered: *Satch!* Abruptly Tim turned toward home plate. Satch was gone. The skull and scattered balls had vanished, too. The soft, well-worn cap with the perfectly curved bill no longer hung on the backstop, and the great overhead lights went dark.

Tim headed home across the outfield, a landscape of stars bending overhead. The game had only been a tie, and Satch still held the baseball cap, a piece of Tim's life, in his grip. Tim knew Satch might return someday, perhaps to finish the game, and he hoped he would be better prepared for the challenge. But this was not the time to worry about the distant day. Tonight was for remembering good times and visiting fond memories in his sleep.

Tomorrow there would be apologies to make, baseball games to play, and brownies to eat.

The Ballad of B.B. Beatty

Guam Independent Zone

October 25, 2031

He stood on the porch of his humble island home, listening to the squeal of seabirds as they swooped down on a school of fish running just off the beach, and watching the tropical wind rustle through the tops of the coconut palms. More than anything he wanted to stay on that porch and feel the warmth of the afternoon sun on his face. But he couldn't do that.

The timer on the Holo Net buzzed, and he knew he had only two minutes left—two minutes before an unwelcome visitor would project herself into his house from a Holo Booth somewhere in Tokyo. Two minutes before he would have to face the music.

He went inside and sat in his recliner chair, but his stomach began to churn, so he got up to pour himself a glass of water. As he passed the sliding door that led to the porch, he shuddered and stopped in his tracks. It was as if the figure in the glass belonged to someone else. His once-thick head of red hair was thinning on top, he was a good

30 pounds overweight, and his clothes were dirty and wrinkled. He closed his eyes and saw a young, lean man posing for a photograph clad in a brightly colored baseball uniform. But then that image began to fade.

In his living room the Holo system was playing an image from an old digital video disk that he'd recorded back when he was 22. It was a picture of the American flag waving in the breeze over Boston's Fenway Park. He'd spent his best times as a boy watching games in that stadium, and it remained his favorite picture. When his Holo system wasn't in use, he usually had it set to fill his walls with Old Glory flying high over the stadium.

The funny thing was, he thought he was going to be safe here, on this two-bit island way out in the middle of nowhere. He thought he was far away from anyone who would light up his face with a Net-Cam and start asking him questions. All those questions. But it was like when you were a kid playing hide-and-seek in the backyard: No matter how well you hid, eventually they found you.

They found him yesterday.

He came in after a short walk on the beach, and a Net Mail transmission was playing over and over from his Holo system like an antique tape loop. It was from Tomiko Kobori, a student researching baseball history, and she wanted to talk to B.B. Beatty. She wasn't requesting his time; she was demanding it. And she knew exactly what he feared most. "Either grant me an interview, or I will Holo Mail your assumed name, address, and Geocode to every journalist worldwide. You will be the lead story on every Netzine within minutes. Do you want that, Mr. Beatty?"

What choice did he have?

His last two minutes of anonymity were up. Old Glory dissolved, and the Holo system started to download incoming data. Its red digital readout counted down five-four-three-two, then the laser projector tracked an array of multiple beams onto an empty spot on his living room floor. The beams grew more intense until they started projecting the image of a woman sitting in a Holo Booth more than a thousand miles away.

She was young, maybe 30, and quite beautiful. She wore one of those platinum film dresses that became so popular with the mainlanders a while back, and every light in the room reflected off it in a kaleidoscope of color. Her hair was striped bright red and black with an animated dye that rippled across her head like a live animal. Beatty could see through her like a ghost in an old movie.

"How did you find me?" he asked.

"If you don't mind, I'll ask the questions, Mr. Beatty." Kobori flipped her hair back from her face with her right hand. He could tell she was speaking modern Japanese by the movement of her lips, but his Holo Net system was set to English. It translated her words and sent them to him in her voice, only in English.

"Good for you," he said, lighting one of his hand-rolled cigarettes.

"I grow this myself," he said, snickering.

"I didn't come here for a list of your vices, Mr. Beatty."

"Good thing. That would take some time, which I don't have."

At first her questions were easy. That told him she knew how to interview people. He recognized that because once, an eternity ago, all the way back at the turn of the century, he had wanted to be a journalist. That was his plan when his baseball career had ended. He wanted to be one of those guys who talked about the game during the Net-cast.

The first rule of an interview was that you asked the soft questions first, then you hit 'em with the hard ones, and if they were still speaking to you, you threw in a few more soft questions and left 'em feelin' good. Those were the rules of the game.

Somebody taught Kobori those rules. And she knew the other rule of interviews, too. She'd done her homework. She knew more about Beatty than his sister. Soon the fluff questions were out of the way—all the background about his childhood and his career. Now, she was getting down to what she really wanted to know. She was getting mean, and he was getting nervous. His palms were wet, and his heart began to hammer in his chest.

"How much were you paid to fix the 2012 World Series?" He reached for his glass and gulped some water. It hit his stomach like hot oil. He looked away from her image and muttered, "It was all in the papers. It was all in the papers."

Her nails drummed against a Plasti-steel console. She heaved a sigh but said nothing. Her image faded away and the Holo Net started projecting row after row of type where her transparent body had been seconds before. It read:

FLASH TRAFFIC—MEDIA ALERT!!! To: Holo Net News Corporation, Chicago. Legendary baseball player William Bart "B.B." Beatty living Agana, Guam Independent Zone (GIZ), under assumed name—Joseph Jackson Rose, Holo Net code Walkin'Wounded 1044 @MicronNetGIZ 45234-9152.

He cringed as the lasers projected the words and numbers in the air before him. Then Kobori reappeared and said, "Your choice, Mr. Beatty. You have fifteen seconds. After that I send this message and your life"—she looked around the room and turned up her nose— "your life, such as it is, will never be the same." She started to count backward. "Fifteen, fourteen, thirteen, twelve, eleven, ten…"

"OK, OK. All right, you win. Just erase that thing." He gulped more water.

"That's better," she said.

"Why is this so important to you?" he asked.

After a brief pause, Kobori explained that she had to do original historic research for her thesis or she wouldn't get her degree and get to teach college students about what it was like to live in the past. Beatty didn't say anything to her, but he felt like saying, "What do you know about living in the past? All I do is live in the past, a past filled with crappy memories."

He stubbed out his cigarette in the ashtray by his chair. She went back to asking those soft, fluffy questions. They discussed his major league record for bases on balls. "That's how you got your nickname?" she asked.

It was a chance for him to think about the good parts of his life again, and it felt good.

"Yeah," he said. "I learned all the way back in junior high school that a walk's as good as a hit. My coach nicknamed me B.B. 'cause that's how you scored a walk on an old paper scorecard."

"Funny how your greatest skill as a player became your undoing."

His stomach knotted, and he felt a stabbing pain deep in his gut. He sucked in his lower lip and slouched deep into his chair. "I don't follow," he said, trying to stall the inevitable.

"That's how they caught you," she said. "You had many chances to walk in that Series, and you didn't walk once. And there you were, one out in the ninth of game five of the 2012 World Series, Boston up by one and the bases loaded. The Boston pitcher had just walked two hitters in front of you, and you swung at a 3–0 pitch and knocked into a double play?"

"I really don't want to talk about that."

"It would be most unfortunate if you didn't."

"You're not going to let up, are you?"

"I've hunted you for years, Mr. Beatty. I'm not going to let you get away."

"Let's get it over with then." He lit another cigarette, inhaled deeply, and blew a column of smoke that rose above Kobori's ghostly image like a searchlight tracking the enemy. "How'd you find me?" he asked again.

"I ask the questions."

"Answer that one, and I'll tell you anything you want to know."

She thought about it a moment, then she said, "Your sister."

"What about my sister?"

"She is Mrs. Evelyn P. Lander, a teacher in Des Moines, North American Economic Zone."

He snickered. "Yeah, North American Economic Zone. Call it what it really is, the United States of America."

"If you wish."

"I wish."

She looked at him like he was a lab specimen. He watched the swirl of light off her dress and felt sick to his stomach.

"So when my sister contacted me, you knew?"

"It wasn't hard. After all, 'Joseph Jackson Rose'? Couldn't you have thought of a better name than a combination of the men involved in baseball's other great scandals—Shoeless Joe Jackson, Pete Rose . . ."

They talked for 20 minutes about his days in the majors. She knew how many walks he had, how many hits, his career batting average (.285), and all the teams he played for and where they finished in the standings. Then she got to the days when he played for the Tokyo Tsunami. That was the year the major leagues became the International Baseball Leagues and went to four leagues, one in what was by then the United States of North America, the Latin American League, the Asian League, and the European League. It was 2010, the year the hypersonic space planes came on line. The hypes could fly a team from New York to Moscow in two hours. The old jet planes took more than 15 hours. When the hypes started flying, a world baseball league was no longer just a pipe dream. It was a reality, albeit a short-lived one.

"I was twenty-five when I first got called up to the majors," he said, his voice quavering.

"And in your entire major league career you never played for a U.S. team? Funny, don't you think? Especially in light of what happened." She was gradually letting on that she knew more than most people about what really happened back in '12.

"I don't follow you. What do you mean by that?" he said, trying to cover his tracks.

She got up out of her chair and walked out of the range of the laser projectors. A minute later she came back and pushed a button on the Plasti-steel console. The Holo system projected an image of a fiftyish man with short gray hair closely cropped to his skull. He was wearing an expensive suit, and he was muscular but getting flabby at the waistline. "You recognize this man, Mr. Beatty?"

"Yeah, I recognize him. Buchanan. Richard Buchanan. He was a gambler."

"He's the man you met the night of October 15, 2012, in the Akasaka Prince Hotel here in Tokyo."

"You know I did. I testified to that in the hearings."

"And ten days later you and three other American-born players on the Tokyo Tsunami helped the Boston Red Sox beat your own team in the World Series."

"That's what they say I did."

"That's what you did do," she said heatedly. "You and the others, you cheated for Boston."

"This is your groundbreaking research? I hate to tell you this, but this is public record, remember? I was banned from baseball. December 1, 2014. Commissioner Espinosa convicted me and threw me out of the game for life. Not that it mattered much. Professional baseball didn't survive the scandal."

"How much did Buchanan pay you to fix the Series? He says fifteen million in old U.S. money."

"Yeah, that's about right," he said, his stomach burning and his palms sweating from the lie.

She drummed her fingers on the Plasti-steel again. "Richard Buchanan killed himself last year."

"My condolences to the widow."

She ignored him. "And you know something odd, Mr. Beatty? I met with him right before he killed himself. He told me something very interesting. It seems Mr. Buchanan never placed a bet on the '12 Series. Doesn't it seem strange to you that Mr. Buchanan would pay you fifteen million dollars to throw the World Series and then forget to place a bet?"

"I said the creep was a gambler. I didn't say he was a *smart* gambler."

"Another strange thing, Mr. Beatty. Buchanan claims he didn't pay you anything to throw the game."

"Well, he was a lyin' dog. He paid me, and I bought this house with the money." He started coughing, one of those hacking chest-wrenching coughs. She waited until he could talk again, and then she kept pitching hardball questions at him.

"Let's say he did pay you. Why on earth would you risk your career for fifteen million dollars when you were making ten million dollars per year? Why would you do that?"

"I had some immediate personal debts."

"I don't think so. What was really discussed that night in the hotel, Mr. Beatty?"

"You wouldn't believe me if I told you."

"Try me."

He got up from his chair, his knees creaking, and walked over to the window and looked out at the ocean. "It was a long time ago."

A frigate bird flew past the house and headed out over Agana. He couldn't look at Kobori's hologram, so he just stared out at the ocean and watched the bird wheel in the tropical wind. "You want the truth?"

She didn't say anything. But the tension was thick in

the room. *She knew*, he thought. He could tell by the dead look in her eyes that she knew everything.

He turned on her. "You know everything, don't you? You already know what happened."

"Mr. Buchanan told me many things, Mr. Beatty. But I want to hear it from you."

An angry tear slid down his cheek. "This isn't just history with you, is it?"

"Who was in your hotel room that night?"

"They're all dead now, except me."

"Then tell me who was there."

He rubbed his chin with his left palm. "Jimmy Ferrera, he was the Tsunami's top relief pitcher. Tyrell Mcphee—"

She cut him off. "Center field. Yes, I know. I can read that in a book. Who was there other than you three?"

"Buchanan."

She heaved a sigh of exasperation. "That's everyone who was there in person. But what about your virtual visitor?"

He felt the blood rush out of his legs. Buchanan must have told her everything.

"Mr. Buchanan carried a briefcase that night, but it wasn't full of money, was it, Mr. Beatty? What was inside?"

"A PV phone."

"A personal video phone. Who called you?"

"I don't have to tell you anything."

"Agreed. Would you prefer talking to the press?" She gave him a look like a hunter gets when a deer tracks into his sites. "Who was on the PV phone, Mr. Beatty?"

He rubbed his forehead. It was slick with sweat. He felt as if he were about to explode. He could keep the secret no longer, so he told her, even though he'd sworn never to tell anyone—even though doing it made him feel like a traitor to a government that didn't even really exist anymore.

"It was Ethan Slater."

The corners of her mouth turned up just perceptibly. "Ethan Slater, senator from the then state of Massachusetts?" she asked, already knowing the answer.

Beatty looked at the floor and nodded.

"What did the senator want?"

"What do you think he wanted? The economy was a shambles, people were rioting, and he was up for reelection. The Boston Red Sox was one of only five teams that hadn't migrated down to Latin America, and the senator wanted them to win."

"He offered you money to intentionally lose the Series. You and Ferrera and Mcphee?"

He clenched his fists so tight he could feel his nails bite into his palms. "There was no money. I didn't make a cent. None of us did. Slater talked about how much the American people needed a boost, some bright, shining moment in a time when everything was going downhill." Beatty passed a hand over his eyes. "No matter how bad I felt about helping kill baseball," he said, "helping destroy something I loved more than life itself, I always took solace in the fact that I did it for America."

"You don't see it, do you, Mr. Beatty?"

"See what?"

"The senator played you for a total sap. He got what he wanted, he even ran for president, and you became one of the most hated men on the planet."

"It was just a game," he mumbled.

"It was more than a game, Mr. Beatty. It was a test of your character, of America's character, and both failed."

He felt all the life drain out of him. He tried to move, but he was numb. "Why, lady? Why? This is ancient history. What do you gain from this?"

She reached down for something and pulled it into the Holo Booth. It was an old-fashioned Holo-Cube, a snapshot. It showed B.B., young and handsome and strong in his Tsunami uniform, flanked by a Japanese man in his 40s and a pretty little girl about ten years old. "This was taken in September of 2012," she said, her voice growing soft and distant. "That's my dad, the little one is me, and I think you recognize the ballplayer." She pressed a button on the back of the cube. Beatty's voice sounded from the cube, clean and youthful. It was a confident, friendly, strong voice, not the deep rasp that it had become. "Hey, this is B.B. Beatty, the Walkin' Man himself, and this message is for my biggest fan, Tomiko, and her dad, Hiroshi."

"You don't remember making this, do you?"

"I made thousands of those for a lot of fans. I—I'm sorry. I don't remember."

"I remember you. You were the scrappiest player in the game. The smallest. The smartest. Nobody hustled like you. Nobody played harder. You were the underdog, and that was what drew me to you." She reached for another Holo-Cube, a portrait of the same little girl in her sailor suit school uniform.

"I was a fat little girl with no friends, an American mother, a Japanese father. I was picked on at school, but I knew that if *you* could overcome being small and be a great

baseball player, I'd be OK, too. You were my idol, and even when the scandal broke, I couldn't believe it."

She pressed a button on the Plasti-steel console, and the image of Beatty testifying at the baseball hearings was projected beside her face. "When you admitted you had fixed the game, I burned all my Holo-Discs of your games, the Tsunami shirts, the hats, the digital posters, everything but this. I kept it to remind me."

He looked at her with a gallows stare. "You really think you hate me, don't you? Believe me, you're an amateur. I am the world's champ when it comes to hating B.B. Beatty."

"I can see that, Mr. Beatty. I'll let you in on a little secret. I was going to transmit your address to HNN no matter whether you gave me an interview or not. Just because I wanted revenge. But now I don't want to do that. It feels wonderful. It feels great not to hate you anymore. Don't worry. I won't tell your secret." She ended the Holo Net transmission.

Beatty looked up to see nothing but the blank white walls of his living room and the glowing readout of the Holo system.

For an hour he sat in his chair and stared at the wall, thinking about the shambles he'd made of his life, and suddenly—unexpectedly—he felt the shroud of guilt that had blanketed him for years slowly lifting. All this time he had feared exposure, and now that someone knew his secret, he was beginning to feel alive again.

He got up out of his chair and walked onto the porch. The sun was going down over the Pacific, and a line of deep purple clouds was moving toward him from the ocean. He imagined the rain the clouds were going to dump on this little island. The rains would be heavy and last for days. And just when it seemed the storm would never blow over, the rain would let up and the sun would poke timidly through the clouds.